TWO BLUE LINES

~~~~~~

JACQUELINE CASSARD

Copyright © 2024 by Jacqueline Cassard

All rights reserved.

No part of this publication may be reproduced, distributed, or transmitted in any form or by any means, including photocopying, recording, or other electronic or mechanical methods, without the prior written permission of the publisher, except as permitted by U.S. copyright law. For permission requests, email contact@jacquelinecassard.com.

ISBN 9798218434717

This is a work of fiction. All of the characters, organizations, and events portrayed in this novel are either products of the author's imagination or are used fictitiously.

Cover art by Ariana Cassard

First Edition: June 2024

For Lindsay and Maura

TWO BLUE LINES

August

One

Tess reached up to her forehead looking for the zipper. She fumbled around like a teenager groping for their beloved phone first thing in the morning, unable to connect her sleepy fingers with the cold metal. Her eyebrows furrowed deeper as she searched.

"Ma'am, passport?" the TSA agent asked the obligatory question for the 622nd time that day, but this time had the power to yank Tess right back down to earth to meet the eyes of this confused woman just trying to do her job.

I look sketchy as hell, Tess thought, scratching the non-existent itch on her forehead as she forced a smile. She extended the hand gripping her passport as the TSA agent skeptically eyed her up and down, seemingly assessing her fitness for international travel.

You cannot, apparently, unzip your old self and step into your new life. Not physically at least, which felt like a design flaw. Thanks for nothing, higher power.

"Tess Olivia Hapley," the agent said in more of a comment than a question.

"That's me!" Tess replied, disproportionately brightly for the interaction.

She had been answering to this name for the last eight years, but it sounded so foreign now. She was no longer a Hapley but didn't feel like she could go back to being Tess Thibeault either. Her last name would have to be sorted. For now, she just felt like Tess, period.

The TSA agent slowly handed her passport back. "To the right," she said, probably shelving the interaction in her mental binder of weird exchanges at the airport that she would download to her friends later at happy hour.

Tess couldn't get over what an absolute child she felt like walking through the airport alone. Here she was in her thirties, flying for the first time by herself. If she thought about it too long the panic started to rise in her chest, up to her throat. Flying had never been her favorite activity, and today she had no hand to squeeze if she got nervous in the seven hours she'd be sitting, waiting, hoping to land.

On second thought—she did have a hand to squeeze. Her own.

In true Tess fashion, she had arrived so early that she still had almost two hours until takeoff. She desperately wished all her books were not safely tucked away in her checked bag and stubbornly refused to take out her phone in protest of appearing like a typical numb millennial unable to sit with her own thoughts. Instead, she sat, silently observing the people around her, wondering what they may be thinking of her as well. She imagined the expression of these strangers if she were to introduce herself to them.

Hi, I'm Tess, no last name. I am a childless, thirty-year-old divorcee. I write books now, I think. I'm headed to France by myself for three months. Why yes, that does sound like a terrible idea. Nice to meet you.

Although Tess was no longer Tess Hapley, Jake was still and would forever be the same Jake Hapley she met on an unseasonably cold October evening during her freshman year at the University of Delaware. They were introduced at a Bible study, the only kind of social event Tess attended during her anti-wild college years. The memory was still so clear: walking in, immediately scanning the room for semi-attractive, dateable Christian boys. After a full sweep, her eyes settled on Jake, her best option. He was talking to a girl who lived on her floor, so she meandered over to prevent poor Angela from making any headway. Tess had staked her claim.

Jake was cute, funny and easy to be around. The friendship blossomed easily, and after several weeks of "just friending," Jake kissed her as they were leaving school to go home for winter break.

For her unwaveringly straight-laced lifestyle, Tess loved to kiss. She craved the stomach drop whenever her lips locked with someone else's, addicted to the rush of adrenaline that shot through her whole body. When Jake inched close enough to kiss her, she braced for the rush that, for whatever foreshadowing she had not recognized in the moment, did not come. The kiss was fine. Jake was fine.

Having a serious boyfriend in college is a bad idea. If Tess knew anything about herself at all, she would have stayed single, maybe dated a bit, but not seriously. The problem is that Tess did not know Tess. No one really knew Tess, because the real Tess was caked in layers upon crusty layers of the person everyone wanted her to be.

If she really was being honest with herself, even now, she barely knew Jake. Yet the Christian community the two were so cozily nestled into throughout college kept them together. There was no reason to break up, no grand feelings or lack of feelings. They were friends who liked to make out which, in their world, was as physical as the intimacy was allowed. Most of their relationship revolved around their weekly Bible study, group hangouts and innocent coffee meetups on campus.

With no clear reason not to—and, with the deeply-instilled pressure to find a husband in college—she pressed on, as though cross-shaped horse blinders were cemented at her periphery at all times.

When Jake proposed, Tess could count on her fingers the number of hours they had actually spent alone. It was so hot that day, as they stood for endless pictures in their caps and gowns celebrating their college graduation.

Beads of sweat poured down Jake's brow as he hit one knee in front of both their families. Her mom shrieked, distracting Tess from the goosebumps that shot up her arm despite the heat. Not good goosebumps, the kind you get in the split second you see a car barreling toward you but can't get out of the way in time.

Yet she accepted the proposal, ready to move on with her fresh new marketing degree and onto whatever beige suburban life awaited her outside of her evangelical college bubble. For whatever Tess knew of herself at the time, this would be fine. Boxes sufficiently checked.

Tess and Jake signed the divorce papers forty-one days before she stepped into this airport. She had expected to feel it in her body the way a gin and tonic hit her in the knees and seeped up to lighten her shoulders and soften her mind. But she felt nothing.

"Okay, but nothing is not a feeling. Like numb? Or just not different?" Tess's best friend, Maria, asked over coffee the day after the signing. She had come down from New York just to be supportive, and Tess was trying her best not to misplace her feelings by treating her dear Maria like a real asshole. Even if she only wanted Maria to lounge with her and tell her she was the best and that every decision she was making right now was perfect.

Tess's eye twitched at this annoyingly probing question. "Nothing" had been her answer. Nothing was what she told Jake, what she told her family and certainly what she had been telling herself each day. Nothing was the answer she had prepared to give, and not having further information was as frustrating to Tess as it was to Maria.

She sighed. "I guess not different." *Also, please shut up.*

Maria squinted and held her gaze six seconds longer than Tess was comfortable with.

She caved. "Not how I thought I would. Not really sad, not even relieved. Just kind of indifferent. I'll keep you posted if I start feeling any feelings."

Maria's face portrayed that she was physically stopping her words from coming out. She could say so many things here—Maria was an attorney, wise as hell and an incomparable friend. But when you've just gotten divorced people don't say what they want to say, or even what they should say. Which, of course, in this instance was *Wake up! You are lying to yourself!* Instead, she went with, "It just seems like a bad time to hole up in a cottage by yourself for months."

Everyone had this concern. Tess had heard it over and over and had certainly debated the choice herself. But this was one thing she knew she needed. And wanted, and deserved, and may never be able to do again.

Even Jo, the undyingly supportive friend, had texted *Let me know if you want a buddy!* just before Tess left. This was not a real offer, as Jo's construction job could not be done remotely, but a passive way of hinting that this *Eat, Pray, Love* trip was not actually a grand idea for a fresh divorcee.

Divorcee. Tess was divorced. The word sounded so foreign, so far away from the statistically fair probability that it would be true in her life at some point. She wished for an easier, quippy one-liner to use, like *Thank God I got away from that monster!*

Divorce would have been easier if Jake was terrible. If he was abusive, manipulative or cheated. He really was just fine. A fatal flaw would have made more sense to walk out on, but their greatest problem was that their life was four walls that she had to squeeze herself to fit into. She could have been just fine forever, but Tess had this terrible itching for more than fine.

She wanted to be herself. As long as she was married to Jake, she knew that wasn't possible.

The wedding was also fine. It felt there was a formula for these things, and theirs was just as fine as the next one. They had gone to ten other weddings that year. It turns out that when your religion requires you to be married to have sex, people are suddenly ready to get married significantly earlier than the rest of the world.

Now, eight years later, more than half of those marriages that started at twenty-two had ended.

Tess hadn't yet sorted what was so stifling about marriage, whether it was Jake or the institution itself. In her world, which had such specific rules, it was never even a question—you pick a person and get married and stay that way until you die.

Life was supposed to go like this:

1. Find a person (of the opposite sex!) and fall in love but DO NOT HAVE SEX.

2. Commit to them forever. Continue not having sex.

3. Get married.

4. Immediately have sex like rabbits until you get pregnant.

5. Raise your kids like it is the only reason you were put on this earth. Keep having sex with your husband whenever

he wants. It's your duty to serve him.

6. Die.

Now, with no rules or set path whatsoever, it wasn't clear to her if she wanted that ever again. Tess had obediently accepted the rules of marriage, as with the rules of everything else.

Having broken free from automatic obedience—and certainly the pressure to accept all rules as fact—she had space to question all of it. Life without a plan is refreshingly freeing. Life without a plan is also, apparently, kind of terrifying. Freedom held as much thrill as it did fear, and this dichotomy presented more discomfort than Tess cared to admit.

The idea of parenthood was even more complicated for Tess than marriage. "Lord bless this couple and their children and every generation to come from this fruitful marriage," her dad had prayed on the microphone at their wedding. Even then, at the peak of her hopefulness and dreamy-eyed vision of their future together, the prayer sent a shiver down her spine.

A few years into marriage, Jake's best friend and his wife had a baby. Tess and Jake brought a tray of (burnt) enchiladas to their house and spent the day cooing over the preciousness of the little girl. She could see it in Jake's eyes that whole afternoon: he wanted to be a dad. Now. She could see it plainly. She also knew for certain that afternoon that she was not ready to be a mom.

All of Jake's hope and excitement poured out of him the minute they got in the car.

"Let's have a baby," he gushed.

"Jake, you spent two hours with a cute, quiet, sleeping newborn. I'm pretty sure we are not ready for actual parenthood."

"I'm ready. I know I'm ready. I know you're ready too. This is what we've always wanted."

You're ready too. Although this was a fair interpretation for Jake to have made based on previous discussions, the comment felt more like an accusation Tess wanted to dispute. They had always talked about having a family, dreamed of the three kids they would raise in a little house in the suburbs of Baltimore.

Four years into their marriage, they were only twenty-six, still adjusting to having a fully formed prefrontal cortex. Tess had never had an inclination that she would feel like this *now*, but her gut reaction was to scream "NO!" Instead, she laughed it off, expecting the baby conversation to die for a while.

It didn't. Jake pressed the topic incessantly, and eventually they agreed to start trying after much trepidation from Tess. Their fertility journey started out rocky, and after three years it ended with such explosive, messy finality that Tess wasn't sure she could ever squeeze herself into the role of motherhood.

If she had to pinpoint a moment that led to her now sitting in a bustling airport on her way to France, it held the smell of burnt enchiladas and seven pounds of a newborn baby nestled in her arms.

As Tess watched people pass by, she found herself making up stories about them, complete with backgrounds and characteristics based on nothing but the person's appearance and her own imagination:

The family with seven suitcases who appeared to be on the brink of collapse was obviously heading to Disney World, the most obnoxious place on earth.

The gorgeous young couple who could not stop kissing had to be on their honeymoon, drenched in the joy of this time as a reprieve from their typically volatile relationship.

The elderly group of men taking bites of sausage and egg muffins in between hearty belly laughs had been best friends their entire lives, and they met up once a year to go on an adventure together, much to the chagrin of their underappreciated wives who sent them off while silently running the house.

As much as this entertained and passed the time for Tess, she cringed at how easy it was for her to judge people and put them in a box based on her incredibly limited understanding and perception of them. She shook her head at herself and how she defaulted to these thoughts, how comfortable it was to label people. All the while she knew firsthand how suffocating it was to live inside a box.

For the first twenty-eight years of her life, Tess could be summed up in just a few words. A big "D" Democrat. Even bigger "C" Christian. Enormous "O" Optimist. And a double capital "G" Good Girl. These were the tenets of her life, a four-part identity that gave her exact guidelines for how to live. Neat little boxes she fit herself into that were predictable, safe and, when she was able to be completely honest with herself, unbearably stifling.

The fragile tower of "right" and "good" Tess had built out of these boxes had never had the most solid foundation, and a career change sent the whole thing tumbling down.

Signing a book deal was not part of Tess's carefully laid out life plan. Creativity didn't exactly spew out of her at her boring non-profit marketing job, but she had always been able to express herself privately through writing. The storage in her Google Drive was nearly full of nonsensical musings that only she could follow. Attributing a phrase, even just a word to a feeling took away its power over her. Writing was her safest haven in her world where feelings were like cockroaches to be stamped out and swept under the rug.

The Google doc that would change her life was never intended to leave its safe home in the cloud. It was born on a Sunday. The pandemic was still in its infancy, and her church met exclusively online. She truly resented the need to have "Hapleys" show up in the black box on the Zoom call, desperate to avoid the text from someone saying *Hey, missed you this morning!* if they didn't join.

There was a piece of this practice that had never sat right with her. The obligation was stifling, but in religion, the more you denied yourself, the closer you were to getting it right. That particular Sunday, she took to her computer to sort out the itching she had to abandon this weekly ritual and call it what it was: bullshit.

It started (as it often does) with admitting her gut belief that homosexuality was, in fact, good and right and natural. She had always cringed when hearing about this topic in a religious context, as if there was any reason God would care where anyone chose to put their love or their bodies.

The next was abortion. She had heard an NPR piece detailing how the infamous Jerry Falwell and other Christian bigshots in the late '70s sought to mobilize religious Americans to political action for the purpose of keeping schools segregated. They had handpicked opposition to gay marriage and abortion rights as the issues they thought they could get people most fired up about to get them to vote conservatively. Prior to this master plan, most Christians were actually in favor of allowing women to choose what was best for them.

Hearing this deliberate manipulation for the purpose of upholding white supremacy through Christianity sickened Tess. The rules about what people could or could not do with their bodies never sat comfortably in hers.

Next were the specific holes in the story of the Bible. The contradictory teachings. The fact that the whole thing sounded like a very silly, poorly-written fantasy novel. As her Google doc snowballed, every paragraph she typed ended with a capitalized exclamation: *I CALL BULLSHIT.*

Before she knew it, Tess had a near anthology of musings, ranging in degrees of heaviness, questioning all the things she had accepted as truth and fact for her whole life. As she picked at the proverbial hem of the cocoon of her belief system that kept her so snugly fit where she thought she belonged, she marveled at how easily it all unraveled.

The conclusion was plain: she did not believe any of this.

When a foundation cracks, it must be repaired to stand strong. Every question Tess asked herself about her beliefs split the foundation of her life a little more. Religion will keep paving over these cracks with synthetic repair like "trust" and "faith" and "He is bigger than us." When Tess gave up the obligation for her name to appear on the weekly Zoom meeting, her cracks weathered to a point of disrepair. The whole house upon which she had built her life came down, little pieces of what she thought was right and good so mangled they were unrecognizable. She found herself feeling painfully alone, freefalling into the pit of questions that had been hiding under her solid foundation.

Tess locked the existence of her Google doc of disbelief in a mental safe in the back of her brain. Having finally admitted these truths to herself she felt like such a fraud, that someone would see through her whenever she was with her family or alone with Jake. No one seemed to notice. Jake had been okay ditching virtual church anyway. He was truly lazy, noncommittal and did not care as much about keeping up an image.

It wasn't until a weekend beach trip with Maria and Jo that August that Tess felt safe enough to pull up the shade a tiny bit, just enough to expose the edge of her questions.

"We haven't been going to church," Tess announced, unprompted as she plunged her toes in the sand.

"Me neither," Maria replied, at the same time Jo admitted "Same."

"It just doesn't do anything for me," Jo added.

The women nodded. This could have been it. An honest admission that they had each broken from the perfectly arranged routine of their lives. The almost-empty hard seltzer in Tess's hand urged her to reveal more.

"I kind of don't know if I'd ever go back," she pushed through. "I find myself disagreeing with so much of what I hear there."

"I've kind of been feeling the same way." Jo sat up, turning to the group. Tess dared herself to meet her eyes. "I just have more questions than answers. A lot of what I thought I believed doesn't really add up anymore. It's like I let myself admit that and then I'm spiraling."

"I think I don't believe any of it," Tess heard herself say out loud without allowing her obsession with her image to stop her. There it was—the gin and tonic hit to her knees that seeped up to her head and released the tension in her lips. She had not said this out loud before and certainly hadn't planned to say it that day. Dipping her toe in honest vulnerability gave her just the buzz she needed to crave more.

Maria had been silent, but the sniffle through sunglass-hidden tears revealed her feelings. "I literally thought it was just me. I have been wanting to talk to you guys about this for so long but felt so ashamed and lonely. Like I'm lost and don't know where to go from here." Jo and Tess simultaneously nodded and the three embraced.

In the months that followed, the bond this conversation started solidified the trio. Loneliness was a distant threat, and the further they deconstructed, the stronger they felt. Not even just religion, but a lifetime of beliefs they held without question came up for debate. The nuance they found in searching for what felt true and right and good inspired somewhat of a personal moral compass than a set of rules they each accepted as fact. Their text threads were a right-winger's nightmare of deconstructing every ism they found constricting, supporting each other in true sisterhood fashion.

Why are some of the least kind and loving people I know also Christians?

Who decides which wine is good and expensive and which wine is shit and cheap?

Why would clothes and colors be gendered?

How do religions claim freedom when they come with written rules and restrictions?

Why are women allowed to show our shoulders, but an upper thigh is scandalous?

Who decided that cinnamon rolls are for breakfast but not cake?

Who picked the absolutely random parts of women's bodies that are to be hairless?

BURN IT ALL DOWN.

The questions and ideas sparked from these texts continued to shape Tess's Google doc, which she had been molding into a more sensical piece of writing. She found safety with her friends to begin rebuilding her foundation. Religion had this secret weapon of playing on one's desire to belong, which kept it going. Breaking that down, connecting with others who shared the same questions, gave Tess the support she needed to peel back her own layers.

With the encouragement of Jo and Maria, she maneuvered her Google doc into a manuscript, developed with the hope of dispelling the loneliness of others who may have the same questions. Influenced by several glasses of wine she submitted a query to some agents and eventually landed her first book deal.

Jake had not taken the news particularly well. She waited over a month to tell him, aware of what this deal could do for both of them.

"I just don't get what they think anybody else would get from this," Jake wondered. In his baseless male confidence, he hadn't even read the book but inserted his uninformed opinion that it was not worthy enough for anyone to read. Tess had pitched the project to him as a book of questions surrounding religion, and neglected to reveal to him that she had, in fact, also found her answers.

Her family was somehow less supportive but torn by the pride they felt in her literary accomplishment. She had been even more evasive and nonspecific in her admission to them than she had been with Jake. *Mom, I wrote a book about the questions I have about religion. Someone wants to publish it. I just wanted you to know.* No one in her family was interested in reading it.

Tess's first book *Right and Good* came out in the spring. Once it was out there, she would not turn back. The taste of freedom in publishing her thoughts and beliefs and doubts was as relieving as a bathroom stop at the end of a road trip when you've been pounding coffee (a feeling she knew well—Jake always drove and never wanted to stop when she had to pee).

Although it was promoted as a guide to deconstructing all beliefs to find what is right and good for you, it gained traction with the ex-vangelical crowd. A popular deconstruction Instagram featured the book and sales exploded. Tess hastily quit her marketing job at a Christian non-profit for more reasons than one and went all-in on writing.

Even with the hate mail she received from some particularly radical believers, her publisher was so pleased that they offered a substantial advance for her second book. There fell the big "C" of Christianity and began her new identity as an author.

The other tenets of her identity followed suit. Her philosophical identity of "Optimist", as her friends lovingly pointed out, was a front for toxic positivity. With the help of a well-suited therapist, she started to address the other feelings, the not-so-cute ones she had always suppressed. As she practiced honesty with herself, she dusted the sand off the truth, and this segment of her identity shifted from optimist to idealist. That was real and true and genuine for Tess; she truly believed the best of all people and situations but ditched the reflex to only acknowledge positivity.

"Democrat" was an easier identifier to expand out of its tiny glass box. She had always been interested in politics after learning about government in elementary school. No seven-year-old cried harder after the hanging chad debacle of 2000 declared that Al Gore would not be the next president. The race in 2016 had her physically ill with anxiety over what a Trump presidency would bring. She cared deeply about policy and leadership in politics but wanted to move away from automatically accepting the answer her party gave her to every question.

She read, she listened, she researched. Her practice of questioning served her well in this area, and she became less of a brand-name democrat, moving to a more progressive, almost socialist mindset. Tess knew she believed in social good for all, in community, in sharing all parts of life with all people. The distance from a political party allowed her to throw her time and money and vote behind her gut, rather than accept a pre-made list of policies and ideas from someone else. Her voter registration remained democratic, but she found herself feeling less stifled by the word and freer to question.

"Good Girl" was a tricky one. Tess was so comfortable defaulting to the black-and-whiteness of good/bad labels. As it turned out, there was significantly more gray, much more nuance to people and choices and behaviors and situations (see above credit to her therapist, Jenny).

No one fit neatly on the good or bad side, which meant neither did she. This was a tough belief to shift, but significantly more freeing once she let go. She craved relief from the pressure to be *good* all the time so that she could be true to herself, but struggled with the discomfort this left when everything wasn't so clear. Parts of herself she had previously labeled as "bad" surfaced, and the work became nonjudgmental acknowledgment of all the parts of her.

Some parts of this self-deconstruction were more fun. Good Girls aren't supposed to curse. Tess had always loved words and how they could express unique thoughts and emotions. Even as a kid curse words intrigued her, partially for their excitement, and partially because she could sometimes find no other way to stress the intensity of what she was feeling without them. Forbidden both in the rigid rules of her home life and in the rigid rules of Christianity among her friends, she found herself screaming "FUCK!!!!" in her head sometimes, soothing the fury she felt but couldn't express.

Of course, even within the rigidity of the rules, she and her friends had found loopholes. One of their favorite songs was "Crazy Bitch" by Buckcherry, absolutely riddled with profanity. They would blast the song in Jo's jeep with the windows down, letting out pent-up urges to utter these forbidden words by scream-singing the song in all its lewdness. Because, of course, singing the words in a song was not against the rules.

Tess worked to replace the need to be good with the need to be herself. Part of this whole identity-shaking process was to figure out who, exactly, that was. She resisted quippy labels she could put on herself, but she knew it when she felt it. Her mind, body and soul communicated peace when she was being her true self.

So, Tess's four-part identity and most of her beliefs toppled, and with them, her marriage, many of her friendships, her relationship with her family, and much of her stability. She wasn't prepared for how little she would have left. Once she metaphorically burned it all down, she had such a shaky pile of ash it felt impossible that she could rebuild a life there. She loved her new job, and Jo and Maria would always be her actual soul mates. But they were in different states, living their lives. Tess now had the freedom to go live hers.

On a cold Tuesday morning, sitting in her tiny mid-divorce apartment drinking shitty coffee, she sat with her lease agreement open, ready to be signed for renewal. Leading with her gut she closed out of the document.

Letting go of her numbness Tess decided to take control of her life. After a quick flight search and twenty minutes on Airbnb, she texted her agent, Edgar, the adrenaline of possibility eclipsing her instinct to ask for permission to run her own life.

Edgar, she typed, letting her fingers lead her mind. *I need to get out of here. I am going to go somewhere so I can write and heal and be. I leave in August.*

Go, querida, he responded almost immediately, as if he had been waiting for this. *Send me the details and we will work it out.*

"Now boarding flight 116 to Paris," the loudspeaker snapped Tess back into her seat in the airport, the holding space between her old life and her future. She picked up her bag and moved toward the gate, intentionally deciding to move forward and see what life held for her on the other side of the ocean.

Two

Seven hours, dozens of pretzels and a generous layer of lavender CBD salve later, Tess found herself returned to the ground.

Her anxiety tended to work overtime when she was in the air, making basic needs like eating actual meals and sleeping impossible. No matter the time or her body's silent screams to succumb to sleep, her mind was stronger. The movies she had downloaded on her phone were not interesting enough to keep her full attention. Instead, she had taken on the daunting task of counting down the miles to land.

Once on the ground, surrounded by the bustle of the airport, Tess felt frozen with culture shock. Binge-watching every season of *Emily in Paris* proved to be poor preparation for this endeavor. Yes, the French seemed to loathe the audacity of Americans to even attempt to exist in their presence. However, this wasn't like the adorable inconveniences Emily faced while dominating the fashion world and sleeping with multiple hot, foreign men.

"*Américaine, t'as oublié tes yeux aujourd'hui?!*" a man yelled at her as she clipped him with her bag, which Tess deemed to mean something along the lines of "you American idiot, watch where the fuck you're going". Why had she dropped French in high school? Her ancestors on the Thibeault side of the family were certainly shaking their heads at her, watching in disappointment from whatever the hell the afterlife actually was.

Tess shuffled out of the walkway to regroup. She tossed her head forward, tied up her long, curly brown hair into an enormous, wild messy bun, and slid on her shitty Amazon sunglasses to hide her panic and attempt to feign confidence.

The limited time until her train left coupled with her limited mental energy proved to be a poor recipe for navigating the French transit system. Even with her ticket confirmation on her phone, Tess felt completely out of her element and vulnerable.

"*La ligne violette vers Bordeaux embarque maintenant au quai trois,*" the loudspeaker blared. *Bordeaux, now* and *three* were all that registered, but it was enough to kick her in the right direction.

By the time Tess found the purple line to Bordeaux, checked and double-checked that it was heading in the right direction, she had to physically leap aboard before the doors closed. Even then, she was riddled with anxiety that she was in the wrong place, going the wrong direction with none of the usual crutches she could fall back on. For now, she'd have to trust her gut.

Most of the seats on the train were filled. She opted for one next to an elegant, elderly French woman in hopes of shoving her AirPods back in and drifting into her comfortable, parasocial relationship with the podcast hosts of *Chatty Broads*.

"*Où allez-vous?*" the woman asked to Tess's disappointment.

"Sorry, my French is not good," Tess lied. Partially true—it wasn't great, but it was good enough for basic conversational interactions.

"Ah. You need to learn. Where are you going?" she asked, in perfect English. No outs at this point, Tess had to engage.

"I'm going to Abzac."

"*Quelle surprise!*" the woman exclaimed as if Tess had just announced a casual vacation to Antarctica. "And what on earth are you going to do there?"

The answer to this question had the power to either launch them into a three-hour conversation or shut it all down at once. Tess's low social battery hoped for the latter.

"I'm a writer, so I'm just going to visit for a few months and work."

"Why Abzac?"

"I don't know, really. It's pretty and off the grid. I'm looking for solitude."

"Well, you'll certainly find it there. My, I can think of so many places you should have gone instead," she rambled. Tess let her, as long as she didn't have to speak more. "Nice, Annecy, Champagne. Anywhere, really. What a very strange choice," the woman said, dripping with judgment. Not that Tess was particularly ruffled about this stranger's opinion of her choices, but there wasn't a ton of follow-up possible in a conversation like this.

"I think it will work out—" Tess managed, just as the woman received a phone call. She loudly answered, seemingly frustrated with the caller and talking more and more passionately in French. This was Tess's opportunity to pop in her earbuds and drown the woman out.

She found that even with her headphones in, she could not distance herself from the woman's conversation. Her lime green ruffled blouse, tight grey Miranda Priestly haircut and jangly bracelets made her impossible to ignore. Words like "*frustrante*" and "*demanderai un paiement*" spat out of her mouth with increasing fury.

This woman Tess had decidedly nicknamed "Blanche" was mad and needed her money! Blanche must have been swindled by a sketchy multi-level marketing scheme. Or teamed up with a greedy bank robber. Maybe she was a part-time dog washer who had been shorted by her most loyal customer.

As Tess spiraled into Blanche's exotic, made-up life, she was finally able to drift off to sleep. In her own dreamland, or, rather, nightmare, she was running.

She started off slow, mad at her feet for making her do this. As she picked up speed, she only got angrier. "STOP!" she yelled, but her feet kept taking her faster, farther. "NO! I'm not ready! I don't want to go!" But her feet wouldn't listen, they just picked up speed. She could feel the rest of her body unable to keep up. Finally, she watched in horror as her joints started disconnecting. It looked like Forrest Gump running his leg braces off, only for her it was her actual legs falling apart and collapsing into a pile of bones.

Tess awoke in a sweat to the sound of a little dog barking. Once she calmed and got her bearings, she realized there was, indeed, a little dog in a carrier on Blanche's lap. The tiny white thing was yipping his head off at Blanche, who could not be bothered, and certainly didn't seem concerned about disrupting anyone else.

"He's so cute," Tess said, reaching her hand out for him to sniff.

Without a thought, Blanche swatted Tess away.

"*Ne touchez pas,*" she said, as if she were scolding her own granddaughter whom she'd asked hundreds of times not to bother the dog. The whole ordeal was so disarming that Tess had to stifle a laugh, tucking her hands under her legs for the remainder of the trip. Blanche clearly needed to get her money.

By the time the train pulled into the station in Coutras, Tess was sure the whole train could hear her stomach growling. She had not considered how and where she would get food, and if she showed up to the estate to find the fridge empty, she would certainly pass out. Once she collected her bags and got herself as far away from Blanche as she could, she rehearsed her question before approaching a friendly-enough-looking man.

"*Excusez-moi, savez-vous où se trouve l'épicerie?*" she asked, feeling pretty proud of herself.

He did not seem as impressed with her as she was with herself.

"*Là,*" he said without looking up, gesturing generally down a narrow street.

"*Merci beaucoup!*" she offered, as he ignored her and lit up a cigarette. She acknowledged the increasing likelihood that she was not going to get anywhere with any French person while here.

The grocery store was, indeed, "*là.*" However, calling it a grocery store was a stretch. It was more like a convenience store, stocking mostly basic household needs with a few food items. At this point, Tess would eat anything. She wandered to the back in search of bread.

"*Une baguette, s'il vous plaît. En fait—quatre baguettes?*" May as well stock up. If nothing else in this country, bread she knew.

She threw a couple of seemingly safe cans into her basket and swiped the least scary-looking bananas. Although her cooking creativity was limited, she wasn't sure even the savviest cook could make something out of the random smattering of items she left with. She'd at least have bread, jam and tea.

Back outside the store, she whipped out the printed map she'd brought, having anticipated the black hole of no phone data she'd encounter once she arrived, exhausted and desperate to make it to the estate. It was a little scary, really, how naked she felt without phone access. For someone who pushed against typical young-person tropes, she sure did use the thing often. The days of printing MapQuest directions seemed ancient, even if that had only been back in high school before she got a smartphone.

Tess held the map up in front of her, scanning the streets to find her place in Coutras. A silly task for a person who couldn't seem to find her place anywhere.

Three

A previous, much more energetic Tess had decided that the three-plus kilometers to the estate from the train station would be a very doable walk. Saddled by her hiking backpack and rolling suitcase, she trekked in the direction of her temporary home, significantly more slowly than she had imagined.

Her feet dragged by the time the estate came fully into view. Their will against gravity waned, and she only progressed forward propelled by her all-encompassing hunger.

The main house was huge, much grander than she imagined. Her innate practicality balked at the fact that *she* would be staying *here* for several months. It seemed almost too beautiful, too magnificent for her.

Ivy crept up the two stories of the main house on the estate, reminding Tess of the house she marveled at every time her mom read her *Madeline*. Even if her own cottage down the road wasn't much bigger than a shoebox, the amenities of this place and her daily view would not soon lose their allure.

Tess was irritated at her own panting as she tried to collect herself at the door. She balled her fist to knock, as if she were squeezing an imaginary lemon, and instead wrung sweat from her fingertips. The image broke her stress with a slight smirk as she breathed deeply and repeated the mantra prescribed by her therapist. *I am safe. I am safe. I am safe.* It was amazing how simple this was, but how quickly and effectively it calmed her nervous system and set her back into her body with her feet firmly on the ground.

Before she could raise her hand again to knock, the door swung open.

Antoinette. She was at least seventy, short, plump and worn. Her gray hair was swept up into a bun except for some sweaty pieces framing her storied face, covered with deep smile and frown lines. She wore a red, polka-dotted apron non-ironically with an actual handprint of flour on the front. Her face held the kind of seriousness mixed with warmth that wasn't quite friendly, which made Tess want to spill her guts to establish a connection that Antoinette would likely never return.

"Tess? *Bonjour*," she stated, further dusting off her hands on her apron.

"Antoinette, *bon…jour*," Tess replied, losing her steam halfway through the word.

Antoinette leaned in and air-kissed her on both cheeks. Tess fumbled through the greeting—she seriously needed to get her French act together. Antoinette stepped back and eyed Tess head to toe, lingering on her black Nikes. *Damnit*, Tess thought. Her mom always said the French judge Americans by their shoes.

"Well, come in," she said, sounding more like an order than an invitation as she turned and headed back to the kitchen. Tess followed obediently, perfectly comfortable following any command she was given.

"Your estate is gorgeous," she offered, following Antoinette like she was the mother duck and Tess was her little duckling.

"It has been in my family for generations," she replied. "I have been here alone since my husband died and it is much for me to take care of. That's part of the reason I like to keep tenants in the cottages. To help…" She trailed off as she turned around, but her eyes lingered on Tess's hands, judging them as if they couldn't possibly be capable of being helpful. "I have another tenant staying in the second cottage in a few weeks. He is looking for solitude, like you. He's come every summer for years now."

"Oh, well I plan to keep to myself as much as I can," Tess responded without thinking through how that would come off. "To work," she added to sound less self-possessed.

Antoinette slowly nodded, looking skeptical, and returned to kneading her dough. "Do you garden?" she asked without looking up.

"Yeah!" Tess was far too enthusiastic. "I mean, I'm sure I have a lot to learn, but I did have a small garden on my apartment balcony at home. My tomatoes and kale came up great, but I had trouble with peppers."

"Yes, you will have a lot to learn. The gardens span the plot between the cottages. I require help with upkeep and you can take whatever you need from it. My other tenant does his best but has no green thumb," she admitted with a hint of a smile.

Tess was riddled with desperation to get Antoinette to like her from the minute she opened the door. This seemed a near-impossible feat and set her right back in the pattern of people-pleasing. *Let it go*, Tess reminded herself. *This is the opposite of what you are supposed to be doing right now*. She had to remove herself.

"Well, I'm happy to do whatever you need." *Get it together, Hapley. Thibeault. Whoever you are.* "I'd love to get settled in if you can point me in the direction of the cottage." *Please.*

"I've cooked, and you look starved. I'll send you to the cottage after dinner," Antoinette said as she continued bustling around. "You can set your luggage in there for now and come grab the settings for the table." She nodded to the next room.

Tess tightened her lips to keep from letting out an audible sigh. She dumped her backpack and suitcase in the next room and returned to the kitchen with a decidedly positive attitude. Extroverts need alone time too, and she had so little energy for small talk with a stranger and navigating French social norms. She'd have to pull her shit together if she was going to make it through dinner without killing herself trying to win over the seemingly hard-to-please Antoinette.

"Take these out to the terrace and come back for the wine," Antoinette ordered, nodding at the tray of plates and utensils. Tess obliged.

The terrace may as well have been a Monet painting. It was hard to process that she'd be staying here for three months, but the sight alone restored an energy in her she knew would see her through dinner. She could not help but break into a dopey, full-faced smile at the view.

A charming wrought iron table sat beneath string lights, surrounded by an arch of bougainvillea, framing the view of the sun setting over the vineyard. A lush flower garden preceded the vineyard, boasting gorgeous blooms of hydrangeas, delphinium and peonies. It appeared that Antoinette had, in fact, no trouble gardening at all.

Tess let out a soft laugh at herself—she had seen pictures of the estate before booking the cottage and shouldn't have been this taken aback. It was obvious that she hadn't pictured any of this as real, as she often had trouble matching her awe with reality.

A clang from the kitchen kicked her back into gear. As awestruck as Tess was, Antoinette didn't seem like the type of person to accept dawdling.

Tess returned to the kitchen for the wine and almost knocked Antoinette straight over as she hurried through the door.

"*Merde!*" the Frenchwoman exclaimed, "Ah, you take the tray and I'll get the wine. I don't care if the food goes down but I'm not risking a tumble with this merlot." Too embarrassed to respond, Tess grabbed the tray and followed outside, eyes cast low in shame.

A woman like Antoinette was the epitome of intimidation to Tess. She obviously had no intention of impressing Tess or making her feel at ease and did not seem like the type of person Tess could win over with her friendly charm. After her initial spiel acquainting Tess with the area, she seemed exclusively focused on her food.

Every attempt at conversation was abruptly shorted by a one-word response, and never followed by a return question.

"How long have you lived here?"

"Long," Antoinette responded between bites without lifting her head.

"Where did you live before here?"

"Montreal."

"Do you have any recommendations for anything fun to do around here?"

"*Non.*"

The message was received—stop asking questions and eat. The evening was so beautiful it seemed insulting to sit in silence, but Tess's depleted social energy accepted the unspoken invitation to forego pleasantries and just focus on the food in front of her.

After demolishing the chicken and potatoes faster than she intended—she really hadn't eaten in twelve hours—Tess lathered some jam on a baguette and audibly moaned with her first bite, forgetting she wasn't alone.

"It's tomato jam," Antoinette said, slightly beaming at how much Tess obviously enjoyed her food. "My *famous* tomato jam. I sell it at the shop down the road. You must take best care of my tomatoes in the garden. I am an old woman. I don't do much anymore, but I do make tomato jam."

Tess's mouth was too full to respond, so she solemnly nodded as if accepting responsibility for an important mission from a military commander. Antoinette continued, like a cat who reserved her attention for those who didn't act like they wanted it.

"When I was a little girl, I would come to visit here from Montreal in the summers. *Ma mémé* taught me to make the jam. Everyone loves to eat the jam, but mostly I love to make the jam. I made it for my husband when we met and he said '*Toi, tu es mon amour pour la vie!*' He asked me to marry him soon after that."

Tess watched Antoinette's mind go back in time as her eyes fixated on the sun setting over the horizon. Afraid to break the moment and taint the bonding, she continued to work on her baguette.

"You can see my heart is sad. My Louis is gone, but my tomato jam lives."

"It is very good," Tess managed.

"I know. Where is your husband?"

The question caught Tess so off-guard she inadvertently tried to swallow a piece of baguette too big and found herself hacking with tears in her eyes for a full minute before recovering.

"He is gone, too," Antoinette concluded from the ordeal.

"Yes. But he is alive. Just no longer with me."

"And I see you are not sad," the woman she just met declared while studying her face.

Tess had to look away to gain her composure and grappled for a response. "I...I don't know what I am. But I am hoping to figure it out. Here, I guess."

"'*L'espoir est le rêve de l'âme éveillé*e,' we say. If you are ready, you will find what you're looking for," she added, unaware of the weight the statement held for Tess. *If you are ready*. Tess was so disconnected, so unaware of where she was in life that she didn't feel ready for anything. Especially not three months alone in a cottage in a foreign country. She made a mental note to call Jo the next day to unpack that.

"Now you are ready for bed. Down the road, less than one kilometer, *le premier gîte à gauche*. Off you go." Antoinette shooed her like a farmer shooing birds out of his field. Subtlety was certainly not her forte.

Tess obediently stood, grabbed her suitcases from inside and headed down the unfamiliar road lit by the tail end of the sunset.

Four

Tess awoke in a strange bed, in a different country, after an uncharacteristically deep sleep. In the light of day, she admired the setup of her temporary home. The stone cottage was certainly charming, containing only what she would really need. Antoinette had promised "pretty much" Wi-Fi, yet Tess only had connection if she pulled a kitchen chair into a corner of the living room by the window. She had assured Maria and Jo that she was safe as soon as she arrived the prior night and now had to alert her family of her status. She texted her brother, Luke, the only family member she still had a semblance of a relationship with.

Made it, she wrote, digging for anything else to say to him. *It's lovely and cozy and I'm really happy I'm here.* Backspace backspace backspace backspace backspace. Nothing sounds less convincing than a literal declaration that you are content. *Talk soon,* she added instead, fully aware of how noncommittal the phrase was. She left her phone and headed to her room to unpack.

Her propensity for practicality served her well in packing for a trip this long. Tess didn't need much and happily cut down her clothes and other necessities to two bags for the full three months. Having found a home for some basic toiletries, one towel and bathing suit, her straw hat and a second pair of shoes, she was just about done.

"Hello, old friend," she greeted her yellow legal pad, an essential for organizing her brain dumps into neat rows. The top page was full of words and numbers, and she needed a prominent place to put such an important document.

She fumbled around the kitchen, looking for a magnet for the fridge. Before she left, she had compiled a loose list of things she wanted to do during her time here.

Tess found that the problem with deconstructing all your thoughts and beliefs is that you end up with a wobbly pile of rubble and no solid foundation to stand on. While Tess had spent ample time studying religions and a range of belief systems, she found that she would rather build her own from the ground up. She needed a foundation but wouldn't accept someone else's list of thoughts and beliefs to shape her. And, as she made her own, she needed to write about the process in time for her deadline. However, self-discovery doesn't work quite as well on a schedule.

So, after excavating the parts of you that have died, what do you do to be whole again? When you've ripped yourself out of the seams of your own life, how do you mend the fraying ends to be secure? This question was top priority, so she worked to come up with an answer.

The result was a list of the things that made her feel like she was in tune with her soul and connected to her own humanity. Her plan, aside from writing, was to stick as closely to this list as she could. The break from outside influence was the main ingredient in this recipe for illumination, and even then, it wasn't lost on Tess that she had created some guidelines for rebuilding her new, "unstructured" life.

The list:

1. Be outside as much as humanly possible

2. Make your own shit

3. Don't plan your weekends

4. Talk out loud

5. Write a poem a day

6. Read

7. Choose tea over wine

8. Maybe try to run again

Overthinking was second nature for Tess, so she tried to create her list based on as much instinct as she could trust. She liked doing these things. Even if they didn't lead to a personal breakthrough, she would at least enjoy herself in France, and hopefully find enough to write about.

She was confident in the first seven items and had years of anecdotal evidence that these things brought her back to herself. Being outside, making stuff, writing poems, drinking tea and reading were immediate serotonin boosters for her. Maria had suggested she add "don't plan your weekends," attempting to break Tess from her structured view of productivity. She had committed to a five-day workweek and wanted to keep the weekends for fun and rest. "Rest is productive," Maria would often say. Tess knew if she didn't have "don't plan" on her to-do list, she would end up planning. The irony was not lost on her.

Her commitment to talking out loud was suggested by her therapist. Out of country, she would no longer be able to have sessions with Jenny and knew her interactions with others would be limited. The idea was that talking out loud may help her come back to herself, recognize how she was feeling and stay connected to the present. No one would be around to hear, but if Tess was honest, she knew she would probably get very weird talking to herself alone for months.

Number 8 came later and did not appear on the initial list she shared with her friends and Jenny. She added and deleted the item more times than she could count, and finally settled on leaving it as long as it started with the word "maybe".

For ten years, running had been like breathing for Tess. It fit perfectly into the landscape of her life. Deny yourself. Strive. Sacrifice. A shudder trickled down her spine thinking back to when she imagined how pleased God would be with her for beating her body. That it made her like Jesus somehow. There was no pleasure for her, just good practice in discipline with meticulous time and distance and heart-rate tracking.

This was one tenet of her life she wasn't sure if she could reconstruct healthily.

Now, standing in the kitchen of her cottage, she admired the list as she pinned it up on the refrigerator. "I can do this," she said aloud, both as a declaration of intent and persuasion to herself that it was true.

It was Sunday, and Tess was not about to break her "no working on weekends" rule on the first day. Her stuff was mostly unpacked. She had no immediate responsibilities and no daily to-do list.

"What do I want to do?" she asked herself, aloud, smirking slightly at the absurdity of how strange it felt to say that. It was lovely outside, and her gut response was to grab her book, make a cup of tea and go sit at the table out by the garden. "Don't mind if I do," she said, this time letting out a laugh with the phrase.

Walking cautiously with her peppermint tea, she threw on her straw hat and headed outside with *On Our Best Behavior: The Seven Deadly Sins and the Price Women Pay to Be Good* by Elise Loehnen. She had just started the book the day before her flight and was already hooked.

The sun and tea and intellectual stimulation had Tess in a euphoric peace. She intermittently paused, looked around and smiled. *This is heaven,* she thought. *There is nothing I want that I don't have. These will be the best three months of my life.* The thought arose with a slight air of "I'll show them!" for the well-intentioned people in her life who had urged her not to go on this trip. Still, even without the crushing pressure of Christianity, she genuinely felt the innate urge to express gratitude and appreciation for the seemingly random "blessings" she found in her life. For now, she felt she was exactly where she needed to be.

Several days, an entire box of tea, minimal writing and two books later, Tess began to feel the itch to expand her horizons from the bliss of simplicity she had enjoyed thus far on this trip. The calm she had created for herself was certainly comfortable, but so far any promising idea was followed by stale writing and mental blocks.

She grappled with her first pang of loneliness as Jo had canceled a Zoom hangout due to last-minute concert tickets her wife brought home that day. The reality of how long three months would actually be set in, and a hint of dread fueled by fear settled in Tess's head.

The discovery of a rusted beach cruiser in the shed beside her cottage unleashed a wider radius of exploration and tempered the feeling that she was trapped. Antoinette hadn't mentioned the bike, and the people pleaser in Tess urged her to walk down the road to the estate to ask before taking it anywhere. She uneasily settled to beg forgiveness instead of permission and took off down the road before she could second-guess herself.

Wind combed through her long hair, straightening it as she pedaled. The roads were fairly flat, and she was in decent shape to venture farther away from her cottage than she had been before.

She traveled the opposite direction she had come in when she arrived at the estate and passed the second cottage on the property before propelling herself deep into the uninhabited countryside.

Her shoulders burned with the warmth from the sun, and the wind tangled her hair into a makeshift ponytail. She felt free and good and herself, something she often did not get from physical activity.

A flashback to high school, riding a roller coaster at night in Hershey Park with her cousins made her laugh out loud. It was the first time she'd been on a roller coaster, and the hot summer night felt magical. She and her cousins sang out loud with glee, forming a core memory of youthful joy she hadn't revisited in years. She wondered if she was capable of the same unabashed joy now in adulthood.

"We're going DOWN, down in an earlier round, sugar we're going down swinging!" she bellowed out into the open road flanked with lavender fields. She could barely continue—not for lack of remembering the words that had been burned into her brain from playing her favorite CD on repeat, but for the sheer joyful laughter that poured out of her as she pedaled. Pushing harder to accelerate faster she sang out the words as if it were 2006 again, ignoring the burn that had developed in her thighs with each push.

Once her brain recognized the signals from her tired legs, she pulled off to the side to break. With no watch or phone, she practiced gauging the time from the sun, connecting with her primal instincts and environment. At this point, she had no idea how far she was from home, and the sun was beginning to set. She gathered a handful of lavender, threw it in her basket, and turned back to head to her cottage.

"I can do this," she said to herself with a smile, finding this was a phrase she needed to hear often. Now, the line felt more like confirmation than persuasion that it was true.

Thus far in her journey, Tess was loving who she was in Abzac.

Five

Tess's mom had been the kind of domestic queen who sewed clothes for her children. Her dad worked well over the required hours for a full workweek, seemingly finding reasons not to come home. He paid the bills and took out the trash, hiding behind a newspaper when he did eventually turn up for dinner.

So, with three children constantly in tow, her mom was left to manage the house and everyone in it. Like a queen in an ill-fated arranged marriage based on necessity rather than love.

When Tess wanted to be a bunny for Halloween, her mother scoured every Jo Ann Fabrics to get the most realistic-looking fur. Tess had watched the fabric fly and marveled at her mom's quick flicks of the wrist to follow the lines. The final product—a fluffy, adorable, perfectly fitting bunny costume—had her hooked.

Tess sat close to her mom as she worked, soaking up skills until she was allowed to try sewing on her own. They crafted small pieces together as she gained confidence, the pinnacle of projects resulting in a complicated, self-designed pattern for her senior prom dress. Even now, sewing with her mom was a reliable memory Tess could conjure that tied her to the woman who now felt like a stranger.

As she grew up, she began to recognize what a labor of love this was from her mom. This level of domesticated perfectionism did not translate into her own DNA, but Tess did value the core of the task. Make your own shit. There was something about knowing she could make her own clothes and provide for herself that made her feel grounded and powerful.

Walking around a thrift store, Tess would sift through used clothes and pillowcases and curtains—whatever fabric she could find to make something new and exciting and hers. This hobby had fallen by the wayside over the years and Tess longed for the satisfaction of holding up a piece she had made. Of wearing it. Of being asked where it's from, and the decadent satisfaction of being able to say it was self-produced.

A sewing machine was certainly not the highest priority in her fairly tight, fast-tracked packing plan. Antoinette's brief welcoming speech had suggested a market called Didier's for "all the things you need." When Tess tried to press for a more concrete description of the place Antoinette cut her off— "*non, all* the things you need." So, Tess pulled out the rusty bike with the flat tire from behind the shed and pedaled her way to Didier's to try her luck at making her own shit.

Antoinette's description of the market was more generous than Tess would have given it. From the outside, it seemed to be a one-stop shop if you were in the market for a broken bird bath, rows of Russian dolls, an excessive number of tomatoes or pashmina scarves. More *nothing* you need than everything you need. Tess's curiosity outweighed her skepticism as she wandered inside.

The frantic, nonsensical display outside did, in fact, properly advertise the heart of the shop inside. She found herself surrounded by a smattering of antiques, actually broken furniture, an entire aisle of paper towels, and a confusingly large section of nautical-themed decor. This was the type of place she would have loved at home, scouring the aisles for senseless nicknacks and allowing her creativity to guide her wallet. Here, she found herself with less of a sense of wonder and more of an annoyance that there didn't seem to be anything resembling the only thing she was actually looking for: a sewing machine.

Tess seemed to be the only sign of life in the store, so turning right back around and leaving was a totally viable option. As she pulled the door open to leave just as quickly as she'd come, a dusty, rusted typewriter in the front window caught her eye and she was sucked back into the comical vortex of randomness that was Didier's.

"*J'attendais que quelqu'un de spécial le remarque*," a voice behind her startled her, breaking the illusion of solitude. She felt the cortisol rush from her ears to her toes and shook her head at how jumpy she had become after being so completely alone.

The voice had come from an older white-haired man not fifteen feet behind her, sitting at the counter behind a cash register. His eyes remained glued to a book he was reading through glasses hanging on to the very tip of his nose.

"*Excusez-moi, désolée. Je ne connais personne ici. Mon français n'est pas bon.*"

"Yes, your French is bad," he replied flatly, setting down his book. He had the same unamused tone as Antoinette, and Tess wondered what was so heavy about being French that people could not be bothered with pleasantries. "You want the typewriter, yes?"

"It's beautiful. I don't think I need it, though."

"You need the things that stop you in your tracks and make you change your direction. I see this typewriter change your course. *Qu'est-ce qui te fait danser dans la rue, chérie?*"

Tess forced a polite smile and shook her head, brushing off the slight annoyance she felt in the pit of her stomach that he continued to speak to her in a language she just told him she did not understand. Nothing made her more uncomfortable and angry than feeling dumb.

"It mean—what makes you dance in the street?" he continued, warming slightly and approaching her. He was about her same height, thin, wearing dirt-crusted pants and a sweater with a hole in the middle of summer. "I see this typewriter catch your eye, and I want to know what make you dance in the street?"

"I don't think I've ever danced in the street. I like the typewriter because I like writing." Tess noted her unease at being alone with this man who seemed to be trying to get at her intimate desires and chose a literal route, skirting her usual friendly flirtiness.

"You need to dance in the street, *chérie,*" he insisted, a serious look in his sparkling blue eyes. "And you need this typewriter. You are the American visiting Antoinette, yes? You buy this and dance in the street and sell it back to me when you leave."

Her discomfort clicked up two notches at his unexplained knowledge of her and his pushy sales technique, but she couldn't ignore that this was a kind gesture and she did, in fact, want to use the typewriter for her daily poems.

"*Combien?*" she asked, attempting to gain back some power with her limited French.

"*Vingt.* And when you leave, I give you *quinze.* We have a deal, *chérie?*"

For all her inherent idealism, Tess felt wildly skeptical of this proposition. The entire exchange had been as jerky and uncomfortable as a baby deer trying to walk for the first time, and she couldn't pinpoint why. For all intents and purposes, the man had been kind, but his permanent frown, referral to her as "*chérie*" and insistence upon her dancing in the street did not add up for Tess. She obviously hesitated before shaking his outreached hand, and his frown flipped up like a light switch as he let out a loud chuckle.

"You wonder of me, I see. I am Didier. This is my shop."

"Tess," she responded, slightly loosening up. She was used to reading people and was surprised at how deeply uneasy she felt being read for a change. Especially by an absolute stranger. "And yes, I'm the American staying at Antoinette's for a while to write."

"And *not* dancing in the street." His chuckle intensified. "What did you come see me for, Tess?"

"I'm looking for a sewing machine, but it doesn't look like you have one."

Didier's smile wilted slightly as his jaw tensed. *"En fait*—I do. It is not for sale, but you can use it while you stay. It was my wife's, *mais*..." His eyes narrowed as he slowly shook his head, as if processing out loud while speaking. "She is deceased. *Alors*, for now it is yours. Let me get it."

"Oh, shit, sorry," Tess fumbled. "I mean, I'm sorry to hear that. I don't want to take your personal belongings if they're not for sale."

"I do not like to see it. So if you can use it I think my wife would be please. And if you are the person to want the typewriter, you are the person to have the sewing machine. A person who makes and give to the world, not take." He lifted the typewriter onto the counter with impressive force and headed out the back door of the shop, promptly ending the discussion and finalizing the decision.

Tess sensed that, for him, the conversation was significantly more meaningful—although this was a common event in her life. People tended to tell her things, feel more comfortable confiding in her than she usually felt, even with her closest people. Strangers would divulge intimate stories and feelings and she would simply listen. She had wondered what it was about her that allowed people this ease, and often sat silent for full minutes, just *feeling* with a person with no plan to respond.

Didier returned with a gorgeous pink Singer, circa the 1970s, cradled gently in his visibly worn hands, lugging both the emotional and physical weight as Tess began to wonder how she would bike back with her bulky loot.

He set the machine down on the counter and laid his finger aside his nose, again seeming to read Tess's mind, and looking like

Saint Nick straight out of *'Twas the Night Before Christmas*. She watched as he dug around in a box behind the cash register before returning with two mismatched men's belts. The treasures this store and this man must hold.

"*Tournez-vous, chérie.* This will get you home."

Tess looked down at the belts, and back up at his increasingly warming face and seemingly permanently furrowed brow, trying to gauge if he was serious. An impossible task with a face like his.

"You are going to strap these to me?"

"*Oui, chérie.* They will tilt the bike, but they will balance you. And you need balance. You will trust me." Against her better judgment, she did.

Didier looped each belt through the sewing machine, and again through the straps of the typewriter carrying bag. He buckled each one and lifted his contraption with masked struggle.

"Out, on the bike and I set you up."

Tess could not contain herself at how absolutely ridiculous this entire ordeal had been and how serious he was. Her laugh escaped her louder than she anticipated. It was Didier's turn to jump this time, followed by his own bellowing laugh that dwarfed hers immediately.

"Haha! I see you are already dancing in the street."

She smiled now, deeply, genuinely as she shrugged her shoulders.

Once she was steadily on the bike, he lifted his contraption over her head and set it down squarely on her shoulders. The machines were certainly heavy at almost thirty pounds each, but the wide belts dispersed the weight enough that she was stable. Her smile was unshakeable at this point, as she realized she was really about to bike all the way back to her cottage with a sewing machine strapped to the front of her and a typewriter on the back.

Didier stepped back, still smiling, obviously pleased with his own resourcefulness. "*Vous avez l'air plus légère quand vous êtes plus lourde. C'est parti, chérie!*" He waved, sending her on her way.

She pushed off, slightly wobbling before steadying under the weight. Heavier, yet somehow lighter.

Six

Tess awoke suddenly, blinking and squinting as the morning light peeked through the gap in her curtains. *Shit.* It was way later than she meant to get up.

The list on her fridge taunted her. Although the original intent was to facilitate freedom, she felt so trapped by the things she wasn't able to do. Her one attempt thus far at sewing had not gone well, to say the least, and she now needed to find somewhere to get a new needle for the machine.

She hadn't cooked anything of note and was mostly living off sandwiches and low-maintenance charcuterie spreads. To be fair, anything on a French baguette tasted good to her, and the creativity and determination to get more adventurous with cooking just wasn't coming through.

Her book was crawling along, and her poem pages held nonsensical fragments that were coming fewer and farther between. She chose wine over tea most days, fell asleep often when she tried to read and hadn't even considered putting her running shoes on.

Her success so far was in being outside, talking out loud, and not planning her first weekend. She fought the urge to count her failures and successes and tried to just be.

The squeaks and thumps of her heavy feet dragging across the wooden floor sent Tess back to memories of high school where her roller-coaster hormones had her in a deep depression. She would sleep late, do nothing and feel like shit. Every day.

Productivity had proved to be a pillar of her joy. When you break it all down, strip away the core beliefs of a capitalistic society, you often find that deifying productivity actually doesn't serve the person as much as it serves upholding said capitalistic society. In order for the machine to work, people have to work.

For Tess, removing that internalized requirement taught her to listen to her body, to rest and to separate her worth from her work. At the bottom of the pile of torn-down beliefs, she found herself still clinging to some. Even with this removal of obligation, Tess still needed to *do* things to enjoy her life. Not for the machine, but for her.

This was a critical building block in the restructuring of her beliefs. One brick at a time she was reimagining the structure of her life, sturdier because it was truer. And this desire to "do" was not going away.

Several consecutive days of painstaking, unproductive writing had drained her and took actual work off the table. Her brain was begging for a break, so she decided it was time for her body to take over.

Antoinette had stopped by a few days earlier and commented on the overgrowth of weeds, challenging Tess's claim that she could, in fact, garden. The fear that she would let Antoinette down buried itself in Tess's soul like a sand crab that she absolutely had to remove by impressing *la madame* with perfectly picked produce. So today would be a garden day in hopes that sunshine would improve her god-awful mood.

Tess's endeavor to be outside as much as possible tended to include wearing as little clothing as possible. Bikini-area exposure was out of the question due to Antoinette's spontaneous visits, but Tess had all but abandoned shoes and undergarments in the vicinity of her cottage. Her straw hat, crookedly sewn terry tank and linen short shorts made up her outside uniform each day, barely ever receiving the washing they deserved. As she sunk deeper into isolation, maintaining her appearance seemed to sink lower on her list of priorities.

A passing glance in the mirror of her bathroom nearly knocked her off her feet as she gasped at her severely unkempt face and hair.

"You ghastly thing!" she scolded herself as she wet her washcloth to rub the actual dirt streak off her cheek.

In her solitude she found herself separating her mind from her body, so she had someone to talk to. This separation sometimes felt eerie, like she could really pull her soul out from her skin. The energy that felt movable was really her; the body she kept it in was just the treasure chest.

She swept her frizzy hair back and threw the knotty mess into a braid. Beneath her straw hat, with her still fairly dirt-smudged face and crow's feet gathered at her eyes, she looked ten years older, like a salt-of-the-earth middle-aged woman.

Her hand inadvertently rose to cradle her own cheek as sadness washed through her. For all she had been through, and learned, and become—she deeply missed who she could have been all this time. The sadness clung to her throat like a long winter scarf, wrapped around several times. She felt it, accepted it, let it pass.

"My, how you've grown," she mused to herself after a moment. *Breathe in the present the truth the now. Breathe out the past.* Her box breaths still required methodical counting, but at least she remembered to do them.

The air outside was uncharacteristically hot and thick, and Tess immediately wished she'd decided to tackle a different task. Her inability to let things go and give up—the exact characteristic that kept her in her marriage far too long—often won her good grades and positive affirmations of "driven," "perseverant," "resilient." In reality, it kept her worn, relentless and terrible at setting boundaries. But today was not the day to give that up after setting her sights on impressing Antoinette.

She pulled on the gardening gloves she'd found in the shed, kneeled in the dirt and got to work. Weeds had nearly taken over the tomato plants, and she was not about to let them win.

Even as soft raindrops started to fall, Tess only got more determined.

"I don't want to do this," she uttered out loud, to absolutely no one. "I don't want to do anything, and I don't want to do nothing. I don't know what to do. My writing sucks."

"I feel lost."

"I'm lonely."

"I feel like I'm spinning in outer space by my fucking self. Nose-diving toward a black hole." Her inhale and exhale got more aggressive as she continued to let her feelings unfold, grasping each weed and yanking more furiously than the last.

"Where is the peace? Where is my zen? Why am I so MAD?!" She was fully yelling now. "I am MAD at Jake! I'm mad we tried to have a baby! I'm MAD at my FAMILY! I am so FUCKING mad at myself!" She had two hands on a giant weed, pulling with her entire body weight until it snapped clean off and she tumbled down backward.

Tess lay for a minute before sitting up, panting, rain rolling off of the curly halo that framed her face and seeping into her shirt. This didn't feel like freedom. None of this was fucking working. She felt as trapped as ever, now just trapped with herself.

A glimmer of the grim realization settled in like the rain clouds seemingly parked over her head as she looked around at the mess of the garden.

Was it really her marriage keeping her trapped? Her religion? Or was it her own innate need to follow rules and do the "right" thing? That she would never be content or satisfied or even, actually, happy? The possibility that the problem was neither Jake nor the constructs by which Tess had lived her life, but that it was self-inflicted, was a theory she couldn't bear to entertain. After all of it, after everything she'd done to break down the walls of her life, could *she* really be her own prison? She felt like a butterfly desperate to fly, whose wings were pinned to a wall.

Once the first tear was released it was impossible to stop. For all her reflecting and practice and annoyingly emotionally intelligent friendships, she could not name what she was feeling in that moment, and therefore could not control it.

A bolt of lightning connected a cloud to the horizon in her line of sight and she felt her mind give up and her body take over. As if out of control of her own limbs, she stood up and started to run.

The road was just warm enough to keep her bare feet moving. One foot in front of the other, she gained speed as she came to the straightaway. The remaining mist from the rain now clung to her body like her own personal cooling cloud, keeping the heat at bay.

"Fuck!" Tess yelped, as a sharp rock pierced her bare foot. The word erupted from deep inside her belly and came out so loud it scared her, as if she had no control over it.

The next thing she knew she was laughing.

Cackling.

Howling.

Tess continued to run faster, exploding with laughter. She wasn't exactly sure why, but something inside her had unlatched and a sea of feeling spilled out. She could feel every inch of her feet. She could feel *everything.*

The energy seemed to pour out of her pure and raw, as she yelped, skipped and roared out loud, letting her body lead. Rocks riddled the road, and her feet sent her in a hard left, away from the road and into an open field. Her legs continued to choose their speed, fluctuating from sprinting, to jumping, to skipping. She periodically glanced down to watch her feet as they made their own decisions, as if her brain had fully left her body to its own devices.

As freeing and good as this all felt, Tess recognized that she was running into a field with no knowledge of the land or how to get back. She turned to get her bearings while running backward, just in time to see a pile of brown curls atop a man pedaling by on a bike. The thought of how this scene would have been perceived by a passerby only made her laugh harder and louder, until her legs gave out and she tumbled into a pile in the grass.

Her laugh had roots and continued to build, mimicking the release of two deeply close friends feeding off each other's giggles. Yet Tess, alone in a field, had no one to bounce off of aside from the two seemingly contrary parts of herself she was desperately trying to merge. Truly letting go, letting whatever was inside of her out to breathe—without trying to micromanage and beautify it—felt like exactly what she'd come here to do.

Without a doubt, this was the freest Tess had ever felt in her life.

Seven

Crusty on the sides
  Soft gluten web at its core
Good the whole way down

The snap and release of each typewriter key was satisfying, even if the poem wasn't.

If it wasn't already obvious, writing haikus about bread confirmed that Tess desperately needed to restock her pantry. Antoinette had recommended an actual grocery store in Coutras, which promised to be better stocked than the convenience store she had initially patronized. Strapped with a few empty totes, Tess pedaled off in hopes of better meeting her body's need for sustenance.

The store was, in fact, an actual grocery store. "God, I hope there's peanut butter," Tess muttered as she parked her bike out front. She knew better, but she could hope.

Inside, a smattering of small white-haired people bobbed around, picking up and putting down every piece of produce available to them. Coutras was certainly a town for the elderly, shrinking the hope that Tess would find a suitable friend during her stay.

She tried to blend into the crowd and follow suit, but with her dark skin, above-average height and wild hair she stuck out like a sore thumb—not solely for her absolute inability to notice a single difference in the lemons she was picking up, sniffing and putting down.

She was reminded of the days she spent in New York City to meet Edgar, always feeling like she looked so deeply out of place. Confidence, as with most things for Tess, could not be faked, and it felt like everyone she encountered knew she had no idea what the hell she was doing.

"*N'y a rien qui vous plaise?*" asked a man she hadn't noticed come up beside her. He, too, stuck out in the sea of elderly. Likely in his mid-thirties, he was quite good-looking, tall, thin with Clark Kent glasses. She must have picked up, sniffed and put down at least a dozen lemons with no end in sight. Depending on how long he'd been standing there, she may have come off either as unbearably picky or that she'd lost her mind.

"*Eh, vous me voyez. Je ne sais pas ce que je fais,*" she responded, reddening.

"No, you don't know what you're doing. *Américaine, oui?*" How was it so obvious? She was pretty sure she had nailed her French response.

"*Oui*. Staying here for a while."

"You need help," he said, breaking into a smile. "I'm Thomas. I will shop with you. Otherwise, I fear you will never make it out of here."

"Tess," she responded, slight sparkle in her eye. He was flirting, right? Either way, she smiled and nodded, accepting attention from anyone under the age of fifty. She'd at least get help figuring out what to buy.

"The lemon should be heavy, not wrinkly, and smell fresh. Try again," he offered. To be honest she was hoping instead he'd just tell her which one was best. She obliged, palming the lemon in a way that seemed slightly too suggestive, and smelling it while he watched. The whole interaction was very meet-cute with an air of sultry.

He navigated her through the produce, keeping his eyes on her and his cheeks wide with a smile. Tess turned on her flirt, which came fairly naturally for her. This was going well.

"How is your English so good?" she asked.

"We all study here. It is helpful to know English wherever you go. And I've been around the world."

"So how did you end up in Coutras? It's beautiful, don't get me wrong, but seems like a kind of sleepy town for a world traveler."

"I manage the hotel. I got a little bored of traveling and wanted a place to stay for a while. So, for now, I'm here. That is sardines." He gestured to the can she had picked up, thinking it was tuna. "Do you like sardines?"

"Nope. I thought it was tuna. What would I do without you! I'm going to have to hire you as my guide for all future shopping trips or I'll be lost."

He smirked, seeming to like the proposition.

"And how long are you here?" Hook, line, sinker.

"A few months. I'm staying at an estate in Abzac."

"Ah, yes, the Abzac estate is lovely. You are a lucky girl to have landed here."

"I think so. So far, I have been very lucky here." She paused to grab a canvas and set of paints, looking for ways to enjoy herself on the weekends without going insane with loneliness. Although, having met Thomas, she wondered if she'd be lonely much longer.

They meandered to the checkout line, him first and then her. He waited for her to pack up her totes, and they exited together. For as much as she had been putting off grocery shopping, this trip definitely seemed worth it.

"So, what are you doing now? Would you like to help me pick out a coffee, too?" she asked, cheekily. She wished he'd asked, but she was bold enough to be the one to make it happen.

"Ah, no. Not for me," he said, still smiling. "Have a good stay, Tess. Bye-bye!" He waltzed off to his car, leaving a completely perplexed and embarrassed Tess standing with heavy totes of food that apparently didn't mean what she thought they meant.

As confident as she could be with men, this cut her down to a very small version of herself. Had she actually read all the signs wrong? Or was this normal in French culture? All she knew was she had to get out of there as soon as possible and recover what she could of her ego.

Back at home, work seemed to be the best option. Tess found it easier to sit and focus on writing when she had something else she was trying to avoid. If she paused, even for a moment, and replayed "Ah, no. Not for me," in her head, her cheeks burned as red as a stop sign. She planned to debrief this interaction with Maria and Jo at some point but wasn't quite ready to laugh about it yet. For now, she used the embarrassment as fuel to write as much as possible and fill her brain with work.

At this point, the book was moving forward steadily. Before she sat down at her laptop to write, she'd mentally play out her ideas. Sometimes that looked like staring off into space, fixing her gaze on something while she let her mind knead and toss around an idea like pizza dough.

When she was at the point where she was ready to put words to those ideas, she was often bursting at the seams. Her fingers flew across the keyboard at impressive speed, pouring out the thoughts she had been ruminating on. This came at the perfect time, as she'd promised Edgar thirty pages by Friday, ahead of their first check-in meeting the following Monday.

"This could not have been about me," she said aloud to herself, interrupting her focus to reflect on the bizarre interaction she'd just encountered. "Or am I totally out of practice? Have I lost my allure? Am I so full of myself that I assumed he'd be into me? Do I even know how to flirt or read someone else's flirting? This is bad, oh boy, this is bad." She stood and went to look at herself in the mirror to assess her objective attractiveness.

It had been work to like the way she looked. Even as a conventionally attractive person, self-image can be a bitch. She'd practiced loving herself, exactly how she was, for years.

"Thomas doesn't get to decide. This has nothing to do with you," she said to herself in the mirror. "I love your brown eyes. And your smile. And your hair. You are lovely to me."

A practice this simple used to feel so odd when her therapist first recommended it. Yet over time, it began to work. It was another way her brain could disconnect from her body, and she could talk to it like it was a different person. Like she'd talk to a friend. Tess found that the easiest way to be kinder to herself was to dissociate a bit and pretend she was talking to someone else. It worked.

Tea on the terrace was a must today. She was ahead of schedule with writing and needed to take a bit of time to process the strange events of her day so far. Outside, with the sun on her face, she imagined she was literally soaking it in. That her cells were drinking water from the sunlight.

"Whatever Thomas thinks of me does not change what I think of myself. I think I am lovely. I think I would love to have coffee with me," she assured herself, too practiced in self-love to let a stranger fully take her power.

"Plus, a fling is the last thing I need right now. I need to be with me and only me." She sipped her tea and drank in more sun, rewriting her bread haiku from earlier.

Outer skin glowing

Soft strong web at her core
Good all the way down

"What do I need right now? What do I need. I feel like I need a miracle. Like magic or something," she mused.

A beautiful quote on the wall of the Baltimore Aquarium popped into her mind. "If there is magic on this planet, it is contained in water." Tomorrow would be the perfect day to start her weekend early and find the lake at the edge of the estate.

Eight

Weekend mode activated; Tess headed down to the lake.

She sat down under four different trees before finally committing and opening up her tote to set up her canvas. Painting had always been Tess's calm. When the feelings were so intense she could no longer keep them inside, they would flow out through her fingers.

Once, Jake had asked if she thought she was an artist. The words were not exactly a question, but more an accusation—she was not a great painter. She laughed it off to mask the sting.

Even without real talent, she loved the act of painting. There was something about the control of the brush, the quick appearance of something where there had been nothing, that felt like she could let go. Most of her paintings had been absolute abstract bullshit. Sometimes she would try to copy another painting, or even paint a whole canvas just one color just to feel the glide of the brush.

Today's attempt at capturing the scene in front of her —actually *trying* to paint in a traditional sense, was a slightly terrifying, exciting endeavor. Tess was deeply uncomfortable doing something she was undeniably bad at.

It took hours? Minutes? Maybe even just seconds to start working. Her concept of time seemed fuzzy in this country. The brush felt like it led her hand into the paint and back to the canvas, into the paint, back to the canvas in an almost motorized way. Little tick marks were adding up, and she seemed to be going for an impressionist-esque technique. The lake looked very little like a lake, the little dock was just a smudge, and the greens and blues didn't exactly look like much of anything.

Her eyes got heavy until she allowed them to close, a practice she had recently begun if only to amuse herself with the absolute nothing-paintings she created without being able to see. The dipping repetition lingered longer as she painted blindly, trying not to interfere with where the brush wanted to go. Her lines swooped longer, drawn out.

She opened her eyes, hoping to amuse herself with the scene she had created. Her canvas was now a muddled mess of ticks and dots of varying shapes and sizes and colors. The greens and blues she had been using around the periphery didn't quite capture the landscape before her, but the blue in the middle resembled water. In the very center, she had inadvertently painted a set of blue lines.

Two blue lines. Tess hadn't even had her eyes open, it seemed to come from her subconscious like it was a part of her DNA. She sat frozen, stuck on the lines as if she were trying to win a staring contest.

"Goddamnit," she uttered, closing her eyes again to let herself go where her subconscious seemed to want her to go.

She was transported back to sitting on the peeling beige laminate floor of the bathroom in the apartment she shared with Jake. The stick of plastic placed on the floor next to her felt so unceremoniously cheap for the significance it held.

She remembered the way her breath sucked in and held in protest as her eyes bored into the tiny screen showing two blue lines. As if refusing to breathe would change the fate sitting next to her.

Two blue lines changed her life. Destroyed the life she had. Made space for the life she wanted. The memory held such a vast range of emotions that Tess rarely allowed herself to go back there. Fear was the prominent feeling, but anger and clarity and relief and envy and guilt were all tangled in there too. Tied up in a little jumbled mass, like the tiny mass of cells inside her uterus.

Just a year prior, sitting on the bathroom floor paralyzed by all those emotions, it had suddenly become so clear what she was going to do. At the crux of all those feelings and the weight of what that day meant, she finally knew what she wanted, as if the lines appeared like invisible ink, revealing the next steps for her life.

Snapping back to the present, Tess pressed on with her painting. She quickly multiplied the strokes over and over to fade the blue lines into the background. Even with layers of paint, she could still see them.

A rustle nearby elicited a sharp breath as Tess peered over the top of her canvas. God, she had gotten used to being alone, but the solitude sparked some fear. Sitting in this discomfort, letting the anxiety wash through her and pass was becoming a ritual. Every wash felt less disrupting, as a cloud passing by above her rather than through her. *I am safe. I am safe. I am safe.* The repetition of her mantra in her head soothed the pricking skin on her arms.

Just as the calm set in, she heard a real sound, definitely not in her head. It was a whistle in the pitch of a bird, but a melody that could only have been human. The whistle grew louder, sweeter and closer. She slowly lifted her head until her eyes could see just over her canvas and confirmed the picture already formed in her head—the whistle was coming from a man with curly brown hair.

Tess froze, eyes darting around her surroundings. The tree that had provided such perfect shade all day also put her just out of view unless he was searching. There was something about his presence that reinforced her calming mantra. *I am safe.* The words felt less necessary, as if they had actually sunk in and taken up residence in her body. Her feet connected to the ground, and she felt solid—not willing to give up this groundedness. So, she remained quiet and prayed the trees would continue as her sanctuary.

The end of the dock took on a new form. He moved less like a man and more like an animal, certainly without any knowledge of being watched. His lean, tanned body was considerably more covered by tattoos than by his short, striped shorts. Tess was glued to the scene as he adjusted his straw hat, took a deep breath and gracefully descended to a seat at the edge of the dock.

She held her position for several minutes, watching him breathe as he tilted his head back to take in the sun. Once she was sure he was not aware of her presence, she went back to her painting. With her focus skewed, she found her strokes taking a different form.

Each touch of the brush to the canvas lingered a little longer, and the lines constructed a dreamier scene than she had been creating. On her canvas, the lake looked ethereal, closer to capturing the feel of the landscape. She felt herself painting more confidently, furiously dipping her brush into her paints with less regard for precision. It felt as though the paintbrush was leading her fingers rather than the other way around.

The corners of her mouth turned up at the exhilaration, with less focus on doing it right and a true feeling of letting go as her brush plunged into the yellow paint. She twirled the brush just above the brown strokes of the dock. The result was not a realistic image she recognized but somehow captured the essence of his presence. She pulled back from the painting and beamed.

When you spend so much time alone for the first time in your life, you don't always readjust to social norms when back in the presence of another person. Tess was made perfectly aware that she was frozen in front of her painting with a dopey grin on her face when a loud call brought her back into her awareness.

"Oi! Is this your lake?"

She had been seen.

The curly brown-haired sunbeam of a man could not only whistle and sing like a bird, but he was now calling to her in a thick British accent. As if he had the audacity to be real on this earth.

"I think it belongs to all of us," she called back and immediately grimaced. This sounded much more like a philosophical declaration that humans do not own nature than an acknowledgment that they were both staying at the same estate. Cringe.

He paused but glazed past it. "What are you making?" he yelled. Yes, he was really making small talk with her fifty yards away. *Not only are we going to acknowledge each other's presence*, she thought, *but we are engaging. My move.*

"I can show you better than I can tell you," she responded.

She could reason that her voice was a little hoarse and that this would be easier than yelling back and forth. But the one thing she could not deny was her urge to be closer to his honey-warm skin.

He shined, like she'd never seen a person shine. She was drawn to him. This moment, this split-second decision to abandon the strict solitude she sought would be significantly more impactful than Tess could have imagined.

From here, everything would change.

Nine

Tess wrapped up her paint set and carefully lifted her canvas from the back. She slung her easel under her arm and disappeared behind the trees. The brown curly-haired man had not invited her to the dock per se, but the unspoken invitation guided her bare feet around the grove of trees to close the gap. As she appeared on the other side and approached the dock, she took in the full sight of him.

He wasn't as tall up close as she'd imagined, but lean, muscular. His tanned skin and bearded scruff gave the impression of earthiness. His ribs boasted a large butterfly tattoo, framed by dozens of smaller tattoos down his arms and legs. Up close his curly brown hair was the least of her worries. Her gaze locked in on his ombre green irises that lightened in the center. Goosebumps crept up her spine.

I am safe. She attempted to calm her nervous system.

Tess thrust her hand forward like a fresh intern on their first day at Capitol Hill, full of precious tenacity, unnecessary professionalism and absolutely no tact.

"I'm Tess," she said, way too loudly.

He looked down at her hand and back up at her face with a playful squint.

"Henry," he responded, as he shook her hand without breaking eye contact or softening his coy smirk. "Whatcha got there?"

It was much hotter out of the shade, and Tess instinctively stuck her tongue out just in time to catch a bead of sweat rolling down her cheek. Yet another acceptable activity in solitude, but she needed to get her shit together if she was going to be around other people. She quickly spun her canvas around to face him to distract from her bizarre lonely-lady behavior.

"I'm not an artist at all," Tess prefaced, "but I just like the feeling of painting. I mostly trash what I make." She tucked a long brown curl behind her ear and kept talking to keep from looking back up into those eyes. "I'm actually a writer. I'm staying alone in the cottage down the road to work on my book." *Alone.* Definitely not an accidental admission.

"Well, writers are certainly artists. This is lovely. The yellow is the best bit," he added.

"I don't really know what it is," Tess lied, "but I like it too."

Henry returned the painting and turned back toward the end of the dock. "Have a seat," he invited as if they had previously decided this was happening. So much for solitude today.

Tess followed him to the ledge and settled with her legs dangling over the edge of the dock.

"Your singing is beautiful. I was by the trees when you came up and didn't want to disturb you." She sounded so robotic. Her brain screamed at itself—*Talk like a person!!*

He glanced at her sideways, continuing to trace the ripples in the water with his toes.

"I make music," he stated, pausing to read her face. "I was wondering if you recognized me, but there is just no good way to ask that question. If the answer is yes, I get nervous that I'm being stalked. If the answer is no, I look like a self-righteous fool." He seemed relieved.

"I don't listen to a lot of current music. Anything I might have heard?" She wondered if this was the right question.

That smirk again. Apparently, she was giving him just what he wanted.

"Possibly. I'll play something for you someday and you tell me." Oh, someday. Someday meant another day. This was going to be a thing. "So, Tess, you're here to write. There's got to be more to that story. Care to elaborate?"

There was, of course, a pre-packaged answer to this question. When strangers probed for any details about her life, Tess could rattle off a cute little summary wrapped in a bow of *please like me and think I'm great*.

Something about the way he asked sounded like he already knew there was a darkness to her that didn't show through her honey-brown eyes perched above a near-constant smile. The ease of that, if he didn't see her as the cheery, surface-level darling, gave her a green light to diverge from her cookie-cutter answer. She sighed and dove in.

"I am a writer...working on my second book. I just got divorced. Abandoned my religion. Had a huge falling out with my family. Lost my house. Most of my friends. Upended my life really. So yes, I am here to write without distraction. I'm also kind of searching for myself? That sounds so cheesy." She breathed to center herself and dove back in. "I guess I've made space to focus on the things that bring out more of me. I have a bad habit of blending in with my surroundings and fitting myself into wherever I am and whoever I am with. Trying to do less of that. So I'm here by myself to just be myself."

She hadn't looked at him through her whole spiel, afraid she'd lose her nerve. When she finally exhaled and allowed herself to turn to him, she immediately regretted spilling her guts.

He was staring at her with eyes so full of tears that the hydrogen bonds were stretched to the limit, just barely keeping the dam from breaking and soaking his face. Only then, she realized hers was already soaked with her own silent tears. She sniffled and turned away.

"Oh my god. I'm so sorry—I didn't mean to dump all of that on you. I haven't ever said it all out loud. I didn't realize how cathartic it would feel to tell the truth." She let out a laugh, pressing her palm to her cheeks to soak up the tears. "Anyway, mostly here to write my book, and casually find my identity. No pressure..." She fumbled to recover. Humor was the easiest defense mechanism for her to reach for, always close by like the chocolate she kept next to her bed. Instant relief every time.

"Don't be sorry!" he exclaimed, so genuinely that her shoulders released a full inch. "That struck a nerve I didn't know I needed either. The whole rebirth process is something very familiar to me. It's shedding your old skin like a snake and seeing what's below when you strip everything away. The issue is, you don't know what's underneath, and it can feel so raw and vulnerable to expose." He sniffed and breathed a perfect box breath as if it was second nature to him and not something he had to force himself to do. Four seconds in, hold for four, four seconds out, hold for four. If only.

"Anyway, I'm a crier by nature," he continued as if Tess had set the stage for unabashed vulnerability that would be the norm for them. "It feels good to feel sad. It just feels good to feel, doesn't it? I have had times in my life where I was so numb I couldn't feel an anvil if it fell on my head. Now everything I feel is a reminder that I'm alive and here and human."

She could count on one hand the number of times she had seen Jake cry. She would need no fingers at all to count how many times he had willingly expressed *feelings* to her.

This was uncharted territory. She subconsciously inched closer to him, as if these admissions warranted less air between them.

"I've never thought about it that way," she pondered. "But that's kind of beautiful. I could save so much time and energy just feeling and not wishing away every not-positive feeling I have."

"Sounds like that might be part of this—I don't want to say identity crisis, but reconnection with yourself. Feelings tell you who you are, what you think and how you're experiencing life. They're just data, and we can use them to learn about ourselves without them controlling us. Please send my therapist two years of session payments for that insight," he grinned, turning back to her.

Thankfully, he also used humor to break up the heavy.

She smiled back and they held their gaze in a way that suggested neither of them was putting on an act. It is uncomfortable to look someone in the eyes for very long when you don't really know them, and they don't really know you. But the level of intimacy and rawness they had reached at the end of this dock in such a short time washed away any awkwardness that would normally accompany such intense eye contact.

Tess mentally registered that this may have been the first time in her life she was not trying to be anyone else or shift to blend into her surroundings like a chameleon.

"Well, that's plenty about me. You said you're making music here—any more to *that* story?" she asked, swatting at a mosquito whirring in her ear.

"Ha. That's the bulk for me. I also enjoy being alone to come back to myself. I work best in seclusion." He flicked a leaf off the dock with his long, intriguing fingers. Tess could not recall a time she had noticed someone's fingers before. "Although I do find it quite easy to be here beside you," he offered, baiting her.

She felt it, but he said it, putting words to the comfort she felt with him, created by the comfort he obviously felt being himself. The words didn't come for her, but she silently affirmed with her eyes and he moved on. "I take it you've met Antoinette?"

"She checks in occasionally," she said, shaking the image of his perfect fingers from her head. "We had dinner my first night, but I had just gotten in and was so jet lagged I didn't talk much. She did have some interesting stories. She's a little hard to read—not sure I'll be invited back to dinner."

He chuckled. "If you're trying to make her like you, you'll never feel confident. But if you got her to talk, you're already in. She doesn't usually give up much and I've known her my whole life. She's an old family friend, grew up in Montreal with my aunt before moving back here. The French aren't the most vulnerable, feeling people."

That, she had picked up on. She had noticed him easily skirting the question, only increasing her curiosity. "Tell me about the music and why I maybe would have already known you." *Out with it.*

The change in his face was slight, but she felt the energy shift and wondered if she should have left it. "I sing." He paused as if he was considering answering with only two words. She waited. "I've always loved music and always loved to sing. It's amazing that I get to do it as my actual job, and a lot of it I love. I don't want to sound ungrateful." He fidgeted with the hem of his shorts.

"I went on tour most of last year. It kind of went to my head. I never wanted to be famous, and I didn't know how to handle it.

I made some really poor choices. I've done a lot of work to come back to myself. And now I'm a little paranoid when I meet people. I don't know if they know anything about me, and if they do, what they know. It can get ugly..." He trailed off. If there was one thing Tess absolutely was, it was patient. She let him sit until he got it all out.

"My label has been lenient with me, but I'm coming up to my deadline for the next album. I came here to work so I can get it done without losing myself again." He nodded as if to punctuate his answer and returned his eyes to hers. Every second of eye contact felt like a test to see who would break first. Tess held her ground, but she lost every time.

"So you are an artist...and a writer," she added.

He smiled and shrugged.

"And *you* are an artist. And a writer. Your turn." It wasn't a question, but his coy expression begged a response.

"Yes, kind of—well, yes. It's a new career for me and a little uncomfortable to hang my hat on quite yet. I published a book of essays talking about deconstructing beliefs—religious, societal, political, philosophical. I wrote it for me, to help me process my own thoughts. I never really intended for it to go anywhere, but I started thinking that maybe others had similar questions, and it would make them feel less alone. I got an agent and the whole thing started snowballing. Now, my publisher wants the next book. So here I am." Tess shifted in her seat. Every word she said rang true, but something programmed deep inside her mind made it hard to confidently say it all. She noted it—a sprout from deep-seated imposter syndrome that came with the female physique as inevitably as a menstrual cycle.

"Ah. So, you are a thinker. Not so much on the feeling, aye. How do you write a sequel to that?" he asked more genuinely than anyone had yet.

Responses from others had sounded more like an accusation; "how do you write a sequel to *that*?!" His interest lacked the judgment she felt so often, and she rebutted with as much comfortable honesty as he had given her.

"I've been researching. Speaking with people, learning about every religion and belief system I can find. And now I have to put it together. To present ideas for reconstructing beliefs after you've torn them all down. It's deeply personal, since, of course, beliefs are completely subjective and there is no right answer. And that's probably the thing I have struggled with the most. The key for me has been rejecting anything that doesn't feel true to me and pushing for more of what resonates as really true. I spent a lot of my life accepting things as fact that didn't actually sit right with me. And I don't want to do that in my writing, to present anything as absolutely true. I just want to talk about all of these experiences and everything I've learned. And my agent really wants me to focus on how I am rebuilding my own beliefs. It's a little hard to navigate since I feel like everyone I talk to and every new thing I learn shifts my beliefs a little bit."

"And I imagine they will continue to change. Very interesting. Well then, Tess, what do you believe right now?" he asked, lifting his chin to face the sun and closing his eyes as if he knew this was not going to be a short, prepared answer.

"I believe there are no fundamentally good or bad people. In my gut, I truly believe in the goodness of all people," she answered almost immediately, surprising even herself. The admission left her vulnerable and open to judgment of her naivete. Even still, she had tried and tried this theory, but found it to be bulletproof. There was not a person she couldn't find goodness in, except, sometimes, herself.

"I believe we're alive for human connection and enjoyment of life," she continued. "I believe we're wired for community. I believe in restoration—of relationships, people, the environment—rather than punishment. I believe change is constant. I believe connection to nature is a huge part of who we are..." She paused here, not quite sure where she was going next. She hadn't spelled it all out like this before and couldn't help but mentally kick herself for not bringing a pen.

"...I certainly believe in a higher power, but struggle to call it God like a person. I think God is more like energy, I guess? It's a little hard to verbalize, but I have definitely identified with some Taoist beliefs." The words continued to stream out of her.

"I believe love is healing. I believe all people are worthy of dignity. I believe women are better at most things than men because we've societally been expected to be..." She trailed off, further surprising herself that she let that one out of her mouth. She froze and glanced at him out of her periphery and caught him nodding, donning the slightest smile.

"And I bet that's just the tip of the iceberg," he said, finally. "It's a pretty good list if you ask me. Which you didn't, and obviously, I'm just a man," he added, cheekily, "but I agree with your agent that you've got to get personal. Human connection—the meaning of life, I believe as well, only really happens when you open yourself to that vulnerability. It's a beautiful endeavor, and I hope you reach a lot of people to dig and figure out what really matters to them and what feels true. I'll be happy to read how this turns out. Certainly piqued my interest." Tess instinctually winced a bit at the pressure of this anticipation.

"Although, I admit, you piqued my interest even from across the lake." He turned to face her head-on. His eyes were so intense, and his approach so direct Tess could barely stand to hold his gaze, but the intimacy they had already built kept her there. "I can't tell you the last time I sat and talked to someone like this. It's ironic to meet you when I'm here to be alone. You're obviously very beautiful, but I've had to learn not to get distracted by every beautiful woman I come across. Something about you is telling me I'd have a hard time staying away from you knowing you're just down the road."

Oof. Tess had to remind herself to exhale, not realizing she had been holding her breath through the whole proposition.

It wasn't a blatant proposition, but he was proposing just the same. Tess could feel a magnetic pull toward him. It would be easy and feel so good to make this something. But Tess, ever stuck between her innate desire to follow rules and her propensity toward freedom, found herself speechless. She turned away and reached to tuck the curl behind her ear out of a fidgety habit, just to find the hair was already secured.

"Henry..." she started. Even then she wasn't sure exactly where her response was headed.

"I see," he conceded, already adept at reading her face.

"I just think we both have so much in our heads already and this would just distract us. I like you, and it would be really nice to have a friend around sometimes. I can't do complete solitude," she added, shaking her head. He wrenched his mouth to the side and slowly nodded.

"Friends," he repeated, as if selling it to himself. "Well, I don't know about you, but I fancy a swim. Come in if you want...I won't look." That cheeky fucking smile, framed by C-shaped dimples stretching from his chin to his eyes. Perfectly carved to fit her hands which, given a will of their own, would grab that beautiful face and cradle it forever. He was going to tempt her, that was a given.

He dove in headfirst, like only a boy would do with no regard for their mother's countless pleas not to dive into water where you can't see the bottom. Tess was game. She had set the standard of friendship, so the pressure was off as long as she could hold to her word. Might as well have fun while denying her body what it really wanted.

She stood and slid the spaghetti straps of her mint green sundress down her shoulders, and it easily fell to the dock. Part of her French summer of freedom included packing absolutely not one bra, due to her belief that women with A-cup breasts actually don't need to shield the world from the sultry potential of seeing their nipples poking through their shirt. This was Europe, after all.

She quickly leaped off the dock a few feet from where Henry was emerging, in case he forgot to keep his word not to look.

Tess had often been described as pretty for her brown eyes on her symmetrical face, olive skin and brunette curls (when tamed of their natural frizz). She waxed and waned on her body image and confidence and was currently in a state where she felt more comfortable in her body than uncomfortable. Quitting her strict running regimen had added a new layer of flesh on her stomach, less defined legs and a shift from muscle to fat in some places. At this realization, she had thrown out her scale and bought bigger pants—deciding that the precious space in her brain was better used on other business than wishing she were different.

Regret flooded her brain as she slid under the water. It was not just chilly, but so cold that she would have to have a scalding hot bath later to thaw her bones.

She stayed under for a few seconds to reset her face in an attempt to surface looking less like Scooby Doo having just seen a ghost. For a second she wished he wasn't there so she could have swum completely naked, but the view of him when she finally came up washed away any desire to be alone.

"Cold!!" she yelled.

"You'll get used to it," he cackled, churning his arms to spin himself in circles. "Lightning round. Do you believe in ghosts?"

"Yes."

"Aliens?"

"Undecided."

"Love at first sight?"

"Hmm. Connection for sure. Love, not so sure." She dove down like she was eight years old again, playing dolphins with her sister.

He pressed on when she finally surfaced again.

"Peanut butter belongs on pancakes?"

"Absolutely."

"People can remain just friends even with attraction?"

Cheeky. Tess splashed at him with a large sweep of her arm and dived back under, deep.

The energy between them felt as strong as lightning, as if someone walking by could visibly see it. They had both endured enough emotional excavation for the day and needed to remain light—close to the surface. Their lighthearted banter ping-ponged as effortlessly as their depth had. He was funny—the absolute Achilles heel of attraction for Tess.

The seaweed crown Henry emerged with sent her into such a full-body laugh that she was thankful to be in the water without having to control her bladder.

This entire scenario was such an absolute joy for Tess. She was so present, in such a beautiful setting, with a beautiful person, that she wished for nothing. Completely in the moment, however many minutes or hours were passing as she just lived. Breathing, laughter and joy flowed through her so easily. This is what she craved in life.

A crack of thunder in the distance brought their awareness to life outside the lake.

"Shit, we should go," Henry said, paddling toward the dock.

The threatening clouds that had previously vignetted her periphery, narrowing her focus to just them and the water, now covered the sky above them. The rain came simultaneously, snapping them out of the dreamland they'd been swimming in and into action.

Henry pulled himself up onto the dock with ease as Tess opted to brave the rocks at the shore, clutching her bare breasts. It was really raining now, and the lightning strikes that she was sure were far off on the horizon appeared much closer. Her cottage was at least a mile up the road.

"Grab your stuff, my house is closer" he yelled through the sheets of rain. "Run!"

This intense energy shift was thrilling, but Tess was slightly uneasy at the time shortening between thunderclaps and lightning strikes as the storm closed in on them. She threw her soaking dress on, grabbed her painting and easel bag and tore off after him, keeping pace when she caught up.

They locked eyes as they jogged, sending an electric jolt so strong Tess paused to confirm she had not actually been struck by lightning.

Ten

The pair burst through the cottage door and seemingly let all their breath out simultaneously. Tess hadn't realized how shallow her breathing was as they were running, a little bit scared but mostly so alive. The warmth of his cottage hit her like a sigh of relief.

A puddle collected at their feet as they stood panting, each grinning ear to ear. She hadn't fully thought through the plan once they got here and couldn't exactly waltz through his house dripping wet.

Henry had come to the same conclusion. "I've got plenty of jumpers—hold tight." He disappeared into his room behind a wood-paneled door by way of a doorknob that looked like it had been opened hundreds of thousands of times.

Goddamnit, jumper is a precious word, Tess thought. It felt like he was throwing everything he had at her without even trying. Like someone had hacked her brain to create a prototype of everything she found attractive and thrown him in front of her at the one time in her life when this was the last thing she was looking for.

Tess took advantage of her inability to move and surveyed the room. The fireplace had clearly been recently used, and the air smelled like a smokey cinnamon.

His cottage was slightly bigger and significantly tidier than hers, giving the impression that he was used to staying somewhere temporarily. The only thing out of place seemed to be his guitar sitting on the floor by the fireplace. Tess made a mental note then and there to never let him lay eyes on the mess *she* was living in.

Henry emerged from the bedroom as he was pulling on a cream cable-knit sweater, sealing up the gap between gray wool pants delicately hanging onto his hips. She watched the butterfly tattoo disappear in what felt like slow motion. The floor squeaked out a high-pitched whine as he ambled toward her, barefoot.

"If you ever need a jumper, I'm your guy," he said, handing her a green knit sweater with matching shorts and a pair of wool socks. "The slightest breeze is the only excuse I need to bundle up."

For someone who looked the way Henry did, it would have been impossible to imagine that *more* clothes could make him look better. The sweater was like an invitation for Tess to come nearer, cuddle up and let herself melt into him. Her dripping dress was the only thing preventing her from jumping into his arms.

"I'm the opposite," Tess heard herself retort without considering where she was going with this. "I'll take any excuse I can to not wear clothes." Her cheeks pricked pink as she realized the insinuation.

Henry's eyebrows shot up at her accidental tease, but he held his response, to Tess's relief. She couldn't risk meeting his eyes as she tiptoed around him, and quickly disappeared behind the bathroom door to change. In her haste, she shut the door harder than she intended and winced at the message she may have sent with her slam.

Her sopping dress fell heavily to the floor as she wrapped herself in a much-needed towel. She turned and met her own eyes in the mirror. She looked as raw as she felt, but in an honest, kind of beautiful way. Her earlier regrets about not putting on makeup faded, and she settled into a staring competition with herself, applying her self-love practice, only slightly wondering what he felt when he looked at her. With a deep breath, she began dressing and mentally preparing to return to the predicament she had created for herself by spending more time with Henry.

When Tess reappeared in her knit set, soaked dress dangling from her fingertips, the energy in the cottage had shifted. Two heavy pours of red wine sat on the counter, and Henry was hunched over a record player in the corner. As he delicately released the needle, a cooing French voice filled the space through what she imagined were his own state-of-the-art speakers.

Tess's eyebrows sprang up this time. This clearly felt like a move.

Henry read her like a book.

"I know—I'm not trying to woo you. This is how I spend most of my evenings here so far. Happy to include a new friend." Even with the best intentions the word "friend" sounded like an obvious joke. "There's a shop in town that sells records, so I've bought up half their stock looking for inspiration." The song was almost painfully beautiful. "I put on some rice. Do you eat curry?"

She nodded, hung her dress up by the fireplace and beelined for the wine. "Can I help you?" she asked halfheartedly, as cooking was at the very top of her list of skills she could not seem to master.

He smiled, the effect of which still had the ability to knock the breath out of her.

"I prefer to work alone, honestly. I wish I could work better on a team, but it strips the art out of it for me. If I have full rein over the kitchen, I lose all inhibition and just get lost in it. It's a little how music can be for me."

"I know what you mean," Tess said as she slid up onto the counter with her legs dangling off. "I write much differently when I'm working with my agent and editor than I do when it's just for me. The people pleaser in me turns off and I get to let my brain go wherever it wants without caring about how anybody else would take it."

His smile widened and dimples deepened. "I can't believe you claimed you're not an artist and said that sentence. You just summed up art as I know it."

A softer pink pricked her cheeks this time and she turned so he wouldn't notice. "I guess I do feel a kind of innate urge to create. Most of what I make would impress no one. But I feel like my soul comes alive when I get to be creative. Definitely like I lose my inhibitions, which I find hard to do in most of my life. Except maybe when I'm running."

Did he have a permanent smile? She recalled her wedding day when her cheeks were spasming from forced smiling so much. Jake had not had the same pressure, but looked a little miserable in their wedding pictures, as if an omen for the road ahead. Henry must have incredible cheek muscles from having to look pleasant all the time in the public eye.

"Ah, yes. I knew it. I think I saw you running the other day. Although I'm not sure I would call it running—more like skipping? And yelling?"

Tess's hand shot to her mouth to stifle an all-out snort. So much for inhibitions—if he had seen her in her absolute rawest moment there was nothing to put on at this point. She decided to lean into the vulnerability.

"Definitely hoped no one had seen that. But yeah, I just started running and kind of lost myself in it. I'm not sure what happened, exactly, but it felt like an emotional dam burst and all of this bottled-up stuff came out. I just started laughing, then crying, I think even screaming at some point? I'm sure that was quite a scene."

He chuckled. "I saw. It was pretty beautiful to watch if I'm honest." He shrugged as he chopped onions at what looked like double speed. "It is rare to see people free enough to be themselves, and that's the sense I got watching you. It sounds a bit creepy now that I stopped to watch you having a very personal moment. I didn't mean to steal that from you." He slid the rainbow of vegetables off the cutting board with a single finger. A warmth spread through her body. "For me, it takes psychedelics to let go like that."

The comfort she had felt with Henry all day translated to this space. She slid down from the counter and tried a cabinet. First try she found bowls and continued to set the table as if she was in her own house.

"I've been working on that pretty hard, and pretty unsuccessfully," she admitted. "It sounds so obviously contradictory now, to work to let go. My instinct is more work. I've been working to fit the world I live in for so long. My marriage, my job, my family, my faith. All of it felt like little boxes I had to shrink myself to squeeze into, so I didn't disrupt anything or anyone. It started to feel like I shrunk myself so small I disappeared." She set the water glasses and sat down with an audible exhale. "I don't know why I keep running off the deep end with you here like you're my personal diary. I've never been by myself this long and didn't realize how much I was missing talking to people in real life."

He brought the pot over and plopped down in the chair across from her. "Happy to oblige. I would take company from just about anyone right now, but I have to say I am delighted it's you. You are a truly exceptional new…friend." His voice dropped out a bit at the last word.

Tess wasn't used to this directness, especially not by way of a compliment. She had never seen herself as exceptional and figured this was just the way he talked to people. At a concert, he had to capture an entire crowd, and he sure had figured out a way to make each individual feel special.

She decided to take it with a grain of salt but couldn't help noticing how beautiful and seen she felt at this comment, in a way she had never before. A mouthwatering spoonful of curry kept her from gushing to him about how this made her feel.

The pair continued the most romantic dinner Tess could have imagined while reveling in each other's company and denying every urge to acknowledge the chemistry between them. As she collected the bowls to wash, she couldn't believe how normal this felt. She felt exactly like herself when she had no need to try to be someone else.

Henry slipped out to the shed for wood to get the fire going, as the day had turned to a chilly night. The unspoken agreement seemed to be that the evening would continue as the fire was set and more wine was poured. Henry switched out the record and the familiar horns of Edith Piaf sent a buzz through Tess's whole body.

"Ugh I love this song," she almost moaned with her eyes closed.

"Dance with me," he offered as he held out his hand. "I promise I'll behave." This seemed to be the plainest lie of the night, as the agreement to be just friends was hanging on by a thread.

Her second glass of wine won and she took his hand. He pulled her up from the floor with impressive ease, as his size did not boast his strength. At just a few inches taller than her their eyes were aligned as they stood face-to-face. Their fingers intertwined and his left arm slid around her waist to hold her in a secure grasp. She wondered if he would slide his hand lower and if she would go crazier if he did or if he didn't.

His sharp jaw rested gently against her cheek. The comfort of his cable knit did not disappoint, although she couldn't help but wonder how this would feel without all the wool between them.

"*Il me dit des mots d'amour, des mots de tous les jours, et me fait quelque chose,*" he softly sang in perfect French as they swayed. She pulled back to look at him and it was more than she could take. His ombre green eyes wiped out any inch of will she had left to fight what was happening. She was here to let go, and she had no choice left at this point but to do just that.

"I think keeping away from you is going to pose more of a distraction. Maybe we need to get this out of our systems?" she asked, only half meaning it.

He raised an eyebrow as his lips gave way to a smile. "I have a feeling I'm not going to be able to get you out of my system. But I'm happy to try if that's what you really want," he said, knowing she was already too far gone to look back.

After a full minute of silently holding each other's gaze, Tess leaned in and let go.

Kissing had always been her favorite expression of affection. Henry's mouth carefully explored hers, expressing genuine interest and intrigue with a subtext of passion. She plunged her hands into the curly locks that had sucked her in from afar, and the reality of their touch did not disappoint. He kissed every inch of her face as they began to remove the wool fibers that separated them.

Henry pulled away and walked toward the fire to sit down. Tess froze in self-consciousness, wondering what she had done wrong. Her naked body visibly tensed, giving her away.

"I just want to see you for a bit. Come sit with me—I don't want to rush," he said as if she would have denied him any request right now.

Tess approached him on the rug and sat down across from him. He casually leaned on one knee, displaying all of himself in front of her without the slightest whiff of self-consciousness. His visible excitement, confidence, and ability to take his time turned her on more than she would have imagined.

Henry's gaze felt like pure admiration. It was rare that a man looked at Tess in a way that didn't feel like he was hungry, selfishly taking something from her that wasn't his. She often felt small when she sat in a man's gaze, but Henry's eyes made her feel bigger and more present. Like she deserved to take up space and be a woman. It was exhilarating.

It felt like forever before he pulled her back into him. She marveled at the contrast of wanting to go slow and look at him longer, juxtaposed with her desperate desire to have all of him immediately. Every place where their skin touched felt electric, gaining passion by the moment.

Her confidence in her sexuality with this near-stranger was a new revelation, trumping the sexual shame she had experienced for much of her life. It felt right and true and good to her.

She leaned into it, trusting her own lead, totally in sync with his.

They silently lay in front of the fire, tangled together in the love they had made. She traced the outline of his butterfly tattoo, unwilling and unable to come down from the high.

Tess had slept with one man while she was separated from Jake. The date had been decent, and she was lonely as hell, so she attempted to live out the sexual liberation she had longed for in her twenties. It was so different from her normal routine with Jake—not better or worse, but certainly not the satisfaction she had hoped she'd feel. He never called again and neither did she.

She had wondered if she actually was the type of person to only sleep with a serious romantic partner, religious guilt or not. She couldn't prevent the smile that broke across her face realizing she was now lying with a man she didn't even know when she had woken up that morning.

"Your face gives you away," he said, coyly.

"Everything about who I am with you has surprised me today. I don't typically sleep with strangers."

He smiled and she realized he probably *did* do this.

"Did it feel right to you?" he asked.

"Sleeping with strangers? Probably not a core component of who I am. Sleeping with you, here, now? That felt surprisingly right."

"And now it's out of your system?" It seemed he intended to ask teasingly, but there was a tinge of accusation. She was quiet for a minute, careful with her next steps.

"One of the boundaries I set for myself here is that I don't write on the weekends. I do the things that bring me joy, bring me back to myself. And this falls into that category for me."

"So I have you for the rest of the weekend then? Is that what you want?"

"I think we could try to get this all out of our system in a weekend," she said, trying cheeky on for size. He laughed.

"If that's what you want, I am sure willing to try," he said, rolling on top of her. Her smile mirrored his and she nodded, content with this agreement for now. She wrapped her legs around him and he put his arms around her waist, pulling her up as he stood.

"Then I'm not wasting a minute," he said, eyes alive as he carried her back into his room behind the wooden door. She threw her head back and laughed with the glee of a woman who has everything she wants. The woman she wanted to be.

Eleven

"We're going to need sustenance," Henry grunted as he rolled over and sat up. To Tess's dreamy post-coital gaze, the morning light contrasting on his back muscles looked like mountains and ravines. Morning sex had never been top of Tess's to-do list, but she really seemed to be taking the task of getting him out of her system seriously.

She could not get enough. They had made love three times in the last twelve hours, a feat she had not come anywhere close to with Jake. Even on their wedding night, with years of pent-up excitement to finally be able to sleep together, she was pretty over it after one time.

"What do you not like? I have a smattering of random food I can throw together, but it may be a bit unconventional. Tea and coffee, of course," he offered as if he were her short-order cook. They had both slept naked, a new and freeing ritual for Tess, and especially enjoyable in his company.

"I'll eat absolutely anything. I'm very easy to please," she smirked, noting the layers of meaning. "I'm a shit cook with very low standards, so I'll take whatever I can get. Let me do the coffee." It was all she could really offer and she wanted to be useful.

"Well look at you," he smiled and leaned down to kiss her, still completely nude with no obvious intention to dress. "I'll have a tea though." How predictably British. And sexy.

"There's lemon balm and mint and chamomile in the garden," she replied, following him into the kitchen. The ease of this regular morning routine, completely naked with a person she met yesterday, could not be a more uncharacteristic activity for Tess.

"Just English Breakfast for me," he nodded at the far cabinet. "Have you spent much time in the garden?"

"Actually, yes. The irony of my complete inability to cook is that I really enjoy gardening. I grow a decent amount of food at home" She filled the old brass kettle and set it on the stove, stiffening as she leaned back onto the cold counter with her bare ass. His stifled laugh gave away his awareness.

"Lucky we've got each other then. I cannot garden for the life of me and tend to kill off half of Antoinette's stock trying to help while I'm here. But whatever you grow, I'll cook."

Tess had to ignore the insinuation that they were a pair so the thought wouldn't take root in her brain. "Lucky," she repeated, although she couldn't think of a more unlucky time to meet a person like him. Queen of control and rules, yet self-aware enough to know she was already in over her head.

They made breakfast side by side as if it were one of hundreds of Saturdays they had practiced this ritual. As freeing as their nudity was, she insisted they throw something on before heading out to the terrace to eat. The possibility of Antoinette seeing them was too uncomfortable to bear.

Henry had indeed whipped up an unconventional concoction of eggs, vegetables and herbs. It had an earthiness to it that she felt when she first saw his face up close. She devoured every bite. He took his time, as it seemed this was Henry's approach to everything good in life.

Tess regretted her American instinct to eat hurriedly, clean up, move to the next thing. Here, they lounged in the morning light, simply enjoying each other's company. Their breakfast conversation varied in importance, yet she clung to his every word and wondered if she'd ever come across a person so thoroughly beautiful before or would ever again.

"Can I ask about your relationships?" he mused, proving his curiosity with a smirk.

"You can, but there isn't enough time in the world for me to explain my expansive dating history," Tess joked, waving her arm in a wide gesture. "But I'll try. See I dated this guy, Jake, who was nice enough. Then I married him and now I'm divorced."

"And that's the whole story?" he remarked, forgetting to hide his incredulous reaction to such a completely bland recounting of romantic history.

"That's the whole story. It could not possibly be more boring."

"And if it wasn't for this Jake who, it seems, simply swept you off your feet—what sort of people would you date?"

Now this was a fair question. Dating exclusively Christian, semi-attractive, available men left such a small dating pool that, once broken from the tight constrictions, the world was wide open. She just hadn't quite had the time and energy yet to venture.

"Certainly not musicians," she poked with a coy smile. "I went on a few dates after Jake and I separated. But I missed the normal 'who do I like' part of my teens and twenties. I don't really know what sort of people I'm interested in. I don't even know if I am exclusively interested in men. I like lots of people, and I often feel connected to people. It kind of feels like I know it when I see it, but it's hard to explain what attracts me. Something about the light in a person."

He nodded, seemingly agreeing. The socially acceptable response is to ask the question back, but delving into Henry's dating history was not exactly appealing. Instead, she headed further down the path she had started to pave, thirsty for more of him.

"Tell me more about your music," she prodded as delicately and unassumingly as she could, allowing him to divulge as much or as little as he wanted.

Henry sighed but obliged. "It was just a hobby for me for a long time. I was working in a record shop in Ipswich and would play in coffee shops and pubs on the weekends. I had a girlfriend, Celine, and a very quiet life. A few years in, an old schoolmate of mine was in town and came to see me. He had a connection at a studio and that's when it really began. The first album came out and nothing really happened. I wanted to go back to the record shop and pubs and whatnot, but my manager had me push through a second album and give in to a more poppy sound than my folky songs. We shook up the band lineup and made the album, and the single got picked up by radio stations all over England." He paused to sip his tea.

"Everything took off from there. We booked the tour dates and my manager kept pushing to add dates as more songs got popular. I went from playing pubs to arenas all over Europe. We even did five in America. It was fun, but it wasn't quite me, if that makes sense. And I wasn't ready for fame at all. I started fucking around in every aspect of my life. I loved performing in the beginning but began to resent it and got sloppy. Celine left me early into the tour as I'd been cheating my arse off. Had an affair with a married woman. Got a DUI. Did some hard drugs and had some nights I do not remember that I'm sure I wouldn't be proud of." He shook his head, as if shaking out the feelings.

"I was so fucking numb, like a shell of a person. One day, I woke up in a field with no memory of how I got there. Called my manager and went to rehab that night. We had to cancel my last two shows. And then I was all over the tabloids. There were pictures of me in the field—I don't know how or who from. The affair came out. Therein began my public downfall." He waved his fingers as if to say, "Ta-da!"

He reached for his teacup, ready to round out the rehashing. "Rehab and therapy saved *me*, but stay tuned to find out if my career is dead. This album is my last shot. So far it's deeper than anything I've made before. I love to dance, so I need to work on my poppy bops." Goddamn—a man who could bear his deepest demons and finish saying "poppy bops" in a British accent with a straight face. Tess was glued.

"So that's the gist of it," he continued. "I don't know what this looks like from here. I've been off social media for months and am blind to what they're saying about me these days or if anyone is even still talking about me at all. I just want to make an album that is real and important to me and true. I guess that rawness, that truth of who I am that you write about is what I'm trying to hold onto. I don't want to get sucked into all of it and lose myself again." He was there, sitting in front of her, but his mind was far off.

"And now, what do you feel?" Tess asked, taking a page out of his book.

He let out a small laugh, coming back down to her. "Scared. Focused. I love to make music people love, that means something to them. But I think now I'm a little more focused on what means something to me. I just don't know if I've lost the right for anyone to listen anymore."

She locked eyes with him, nodding.

"You know, Tess, you get really quiet sometimes," he continued, and her body tensed at the notion she could have turned him off. "Most people listen to talk, thinking about what they're going to say next. You seem to listen to understand. When I talk to you, it feels like you feel with me. I don't know if you've heard that from other people before. Somehow it is equally disarming as it is comforting," he finished, hinting at a smile.

She had. It had been one of Jake's greatest grievances with her. "Just say something!" he would yell, desperate not to have to reveal much of himself. The contrast of this experience with Henry's appreciation hit her so hard in the chest, that it nearly knocked the wind out of her. He gave her time as she pondered before responding.

"I think people often need space to get it all out. And sometimes I don't have anything to say, so I just keep listening. When people reveal themselves to me I think the most important thing I can do is listen and give them space." She shrugged, never having seen this as a positive trait.

"Well, I'm glad. I have a couple of songs I've been working on, but there's one I really love, and I'd like to hear your thoughts. It's a bit darker than what I usually write. Can I play it for you?"

She nodded, a soft smile breaking out across her face at the trust and value he seemed to place in her. They collected their dishes and headed back inside.

Henry hunched over his keyboard, looking like the *Phantom of the Opera*. He seemed so at home, yet so invested in his work. Like a mad scientist. His intriguing fingers danced across the keys and the immediate sadness of the song caused Tess to instinctively slouch in her seat as if physically weighed down with the emotion.

Henry played and sang. His song was indeed sad and seemed to dance around his time in rehab without blatantly naming the experience. Tess oscillated between closing her eyes, getting lost in the melody, and staring at him so naturally in his element. He was obviously an artist, and this song beautifully navigated the line between enjoyable music and deep, raw personal revelation.

He sang of hurt and loss and heartbreak. She listened through his melodic pain and displeasure with himself, hearing his aching to return to his natural state. This, if anything, Tess could relate to, and this time it was her falling tears that matched his.

Henry had kept his eyes closed through the whole song to the end and looked slightly alarmed when he finally opened them. Tess returned the eye contact but could barely make out his outline through her tears. She quickly tried to wipe them away, to gush about the stark beauty and importance of this song, but he beat her to the first word.

"It is sad," he said, breaking out in a smile as his tears continued to fall. "But I'm sad. I don't know how an arena of people would feel about hearing it, but I just feel like I need to sing it."

"You need to sing it," Tess replied, hurriedly. "It's heartbreaking, but God, I know what that feels like. The melody, the words, it speaks to hurt I think everyone feels at some point or another. And, like you said, feeling reminds us that we're here. It's not a bop but it gives me music and words and space to feel what I do feel. And if that's what you give to people, I think that's a far more important contribution than a boppy song they can dance to."

He seemed to drink in her words with a solemn face, letting them settle. She felt with him, letting his sad settle in her. Energy exchanging through their gaze.

After a minute, he moved from the keyboard over toward her, took her face in his hands and kissed her deeply.

As the sun passed the midpoint in the sky, they headed outside to try their hands in the garden. They moseyed along the rows of plants, as Tess briefed Henry on best care practices for each species. She could feel her enthusiasm building as he let her talk, hanging on to her words like they were opening doors for him to a new world. Nature sparked an unmatched reverence, melding scientific explanation and systems paired with the pure artistry and incomprehensible magic of life.

Tess was in the middle of a lesson on pruning that she was taking very seriously when she looked up to find her student completely distracted and absolutely drinking her in.

"What?" she asked, holding both curiosity and trepidation in her question. The reappearance of his dimples melted the fear.

"You're like a bloody sunbeam. Just so bright and good inside, and you...you light up."

"I am not all sunshine and rainbows you know," she retorted almost defensively, reaching up to tuck her curl.

He beat her to it, gently pushing the hair behind her ear. Her mom used to do this, and she hated it. It used to feel condescending, controlling, like a reminder that to her she'd always be a little girl with no power. Henry, on the other hand, made her feel seen, more powerful than ever.

"I know," he cooed in a voice so sweet it sounded like a song. "I didn't say you are perfect; I just find you to be so completely yourself that you shine. And unless you are absolutely fooling me, the real you is exquisite." He took a step back, really looking at her with a kind of awe. "That's what feels like looking straight into the sun. You don't have to *be* good all the time, but being you is good." He shook his head as she fought the urge to break the moment. "You believe in good in all people for Christ's sake. That's the real you. It's…impactful to be around."

Were other women comfortable with this level of direct, specific, full-eye contact flattery? This was uncharted territory for Tess, and she continued to fight to stay in the moment, not to dodge the discomfort.

He was right that she had been completely, refreshingly, surprisingly herself with him when he'd been a total stranger just days before. The lack of a show, of seeking approval, of morphing and squeezing to fit herself into whatever version of a person she thought he'd like best was like walking free for the first time when she'd been shackled all her life.

And yet, she wasn't ready to reveal all of herself to him. For now, she'd let him revel in the truth about her that he saw as good. She shook her head, smiling, and returned to the plant.

"Well wait until you hear all my terrible dark secrets. Like that I might just call it a weekend right now and head home if you don't bathe yourself soon. I can smell you from here," she teased.

"Oi!" He came toward her and lifted her to his hips with such ease she felt she might be thrust straight up to the sky had she not thrown her arms around his neck. A sound of pure glee escaped her, stoking the fire in his wild eyes.

"I'm not wasting a second of this weekend with you. If I have to go, you're coming in with me," he breathed onto her lips before enveloping them with his own. The pressure to finish the gardening work was no match for the pressure of his hips on hers.

After the giggliest shower of Tess's life, it was back to the kitchen.

"I was going to go out tomorrow," Henry said over the sizzle of butter in his pan, laying the groundwork for another phenomenal dinner. "Care to join me? We could bike." Even though they had promised the weekend to each other, the checking in to respect her time and desires was something Tess needed more than she'd realized.

She kissed his bare shoulder as she passed behind him and nodded in agreement. Every question he asked, every plan made Tess feel equally alive in the moment and dreading the end. The notion that she'd get him out of her system was well-intentioned at the time, but just plain laughable at this point.

"To the market and Didier's, of course. You've been?" he asked.

"Yeah—he's quite a character. His shop seems to have everything but somehow, at the same time, nothing?"

His sweet laugh. "Not usually whatever you think you're looking for, but somehow exactly what you need. It's like a portal into your own mind in that place. He started stocking jasmine rice for me, so I usually go for that and end up with a crate full of absolute shit."

"He sold me a typewriter and a sewing machine—which, to his credit, was exactly what I was looking for. I couldn't figure out how to get them back to my cottage so he strapped the sewing machine to the front of me and the typewriter to the back with belts so I could bike home and laughed at me the whole way out."

This time Henry's laugh boomed so loud Tess jumped and knocked over the wine glass she had started to pour. It shattered on the floor, wine spilling everywhere. He continued laughing, similar to how Didier had done, and swiftly altered his course to begin cleaning up without the slightest brisk at her blunder.

Tess was frozen with overstimulation—the deep sound of his laugh, the shattered glass by her feet, the wine splatters on her legs. Her body was there but her mind instinctively visited years prior, when a shattered wine glass had sent Jake into a fit. *"Jesus, Tess!"* he had yelled as if she'd committed a murder. In that world, not being "on," letting down her guard to reveal her humanity felt exactly that.

Henry seemed to sense the energy shift. "Where are you, Tess?" he asked, standing to meet her eyes with genuine curiosity.

"Shit. Sorry. That was so dumb."

He slipped an arm around her waist and pulled her close.

"You're very sexy when you're human, you know."

She closed her eyes and visualized how she felt: as if she were swaying in a hammock above a stream. Like he held her up, supporting her full, relaxed weight, but that she was free enough to swing.

Dinner turned into a music session, as Henry's inspiration could not be planned, and, when it struck, could not be stopped.

Tess had distinguished his three different laughs and became addicted to each one. His sweet, admiring chuckle when he was captivated by her. His joyful, childish giggle when something amused him. And his deep, full belly booming laugh that signaled abandon to the moment, to her and to himself. She mused about how these could all be captured in lyrics with a melody, and how the world would listen.

The notes he hammered out on his keyboard were so catchy, Tess was compelled to move. Her shoulders started to shimmy with the rhythm, followed by her head bobbing, instinctually. She let the melody seep into her body, wiggling around without reservation.

Henry watched, playing louder, more confidently. It only ignited the rhythm in Tess until she was standing, letting her whole body move to the song. She closed her eyes, further letting go, moving as if she were alone.

She wanted to be higher. Get bigger.

Once she got one foot up on the sofa, she launched herself up. At this point she was jumping, whipping her hair around, fully giving in to the beat. Henry played the same chords over and over, louder and louder. Tess danced around like a child, hopping from cushion to cushion, shoulders swaying as she laughed.

When it was over, she plopped back down, breathless, high off the joy of doing something she was never allowed to do as a child.

Henry matched her breathless joy with his own awe, eyes as wide as his smile.

"Play me another one, I want to dance on the bed!" she yelled as she hopped up and ran toward the bedroom. He followed her like a moth to the flame.

Morning light projected long shadows on the hardwoods as they packed up to head out into the real world. Tess insisted she run to her cottage to grab her bike and a change of clothes, although most of their weekend thus far had not required any at all. She had tried to stall him at the door, away from the reality of her untidy den, but he was undeterred.

"I love it. It's so...unexpected. I'm intrigued," he'd said upon entering, releasing his admiring chuckle. Her shoulders released another quarter inch at his consistent acceptance of her. The more she revealed and the less she tried the easier she breathed, as if she was settling deeper into herself. She had even slept soundly the previous night next to him, something she rarely did on her own and never did next to anyone else.

Riding side by side, Tess marveled at the trajectory of the last few days. The curly brown-haired mirage atop a bike she had seen pedaling by her was now a real person next to her. It felt right, although her jaw slightly clenched at the thought of having to explain this to anyone else. Her friends would want to fly out, have her mental state assessed and insist that she come back down to earth.

"*Dada da da, da dada da da,*" he sang over and over as they pedaled, mimicking the tune he'd played the night before. Tess joined in. The melody felt like them in song form.

The open-air market was surprisingly empty for such a gorgeous day. They lazily perused, stopping at every stand to try something. Henry was slowly assembling a curated array of rainbow-colored produce—yellow squash from one stand, green kale from another, the reddest strawberries and purplest aubergines. He did seem to have a sense for these things, carefully touching and smelling and turning over each piece to be sure he was picking the exact one he needed.

All Tess knew was that she could get used to this, watching his beautiful mind turn as he made anything look like art. That, and the dinner she would eat that night would be divine.

Henry seemed to follow his heart around the market, without the set plan Tess certainly would have devised before arriving to ensure she shopped as efficiently as possible.

She probably would have minded the exceptional amount of time they spent there had it not been for the chills that shot up her spine when his hand found the small of her back or the amusement in watching every vendor fall in love with him. A young soap maker visibly pushed her arms together to boost her cleavage as she had Henry lean forward and sniff the lavender soap she held out for him. He smiled at her charmingly and bought the soap, and Tess had to hide her smile for the whole interaction.

She would, of course, be the one who got to breathe in his lavender skin later.

Didier was smoking in front of his shop, waiting as if the geese that had been flying overhead along their ride had warned him of the newly minted — though temporary — blissful couple coming his way. His wrinkled mouth curled up into a smile as they stopped their bikes next to him, cigarette still gripped in his teeth.

"Ah, *les joues roses et les cheveux en bataille d'un couple amoureux. Et vous venez apporter cet amour dans ma boutique, hein? Que, j'ai de la chance!*" His grin stayed put as he leaned in to kiss Henry's cheeks. Tess caught very little of his mumbled greeting, but knew enough to pick out "love."

"*Que vous avez de la veine,*" Henry quipped, returning a smile slightly more bashful.

Didier turned his knowing eyes to Tess. "*Et vous, mon amie rougissante.* I see you made it home in one piece and found yourself this man. Lucky for you, *il est bon.*" He is good. That she knew. "What brings you to me this day?"

"Rice, of course, and the rest we'll decide when we see it," Henry responded, confident as a soldier reporting for duty.

"I know what you need." He spat his cigarette to the ground and stomped it out, leaving them standing outside. Henry winked at Tess as he breezed past her to follow him inside and her breath caught in her chest.

Henry's long fingers brushed hers as they ambled down the aisles. They were not a formal couple, and she wasn't about to walk around holding hands with him and risk having to explain the arrangement to Didier. The attempt to look like friends in public when they had shared such intimate moments all weekend sent her heart racing. Even if their "secret" was written all over their faces, the physical restraint was thrilling.

Didier reappeared with a stack of records he set on the counter.

"I give you first pick. You can have what you want, but not all. I have other customers, you know."

"*Oui, bien sûr,*" Henry responded as he lazily made his way over. "Tess here could use some new music to take back to her cottage." The reminder that she indeed had her own cottage she would be returning to shortly felt like it cut her clear in half.

"I didn't even know my record player worked," she replied, realizing she had not yet spoken since they arrived at Didier's. Henry's presence felt like it spoke for both of them.

"You might need this young man to help it work, but I see he will be more than willing to help."

The corners of Didier's mouth appeared to be permanently curled to the sky, as if he were so tickled by the thought of their proximity romance that he couldn't keep a straight face, no matter how hard he tried. Tess wondered how many others had been through this same charade, that maybe Didier's giddiness was more of an inside joke at another fling. That Antoinette and Didier—these pillars of Henry's summers—stood strong and tall here in Abzac, while shimmery mirages of his annual romantic interests passed through like intermittent summer rainstorms.

Although that *was* the plan—to drift in and drift right out of his life—the thought of it stung a little too much for her comfort.

The light outside was quickly disappearing, and their mission to obtain rice and whatever else was running short. Henry thanked

Didier for giving him first pick at the records, as always, and although they only took three, Didier promised they were the best ones.

"*Au revoir.*" Didier waved as they pushed off on their bikes back down the road. "*Et chérie, je vois que vous avez trouvé ce qui vous fait danser dans la rue!*" He was right—she *had* found what made her dance in the street.

The ride back to Henry's cottage was quiet except for the squeak of their tires and some chirping cicadas. A haze of solemnity had settled over them as the sun set, illustrating the end of this weekend for them. The sun rises again, but their romance truly was ending. The knowledge that she and Henry would actually be ending sat so heavy in Tess's chest she had to push her arms hard on her handlebars to keep her balance. He said nothing, but his silence indicated that he felt it too.

Back at the house they worked in their comfortable routine of putting dinner together, mostly quiet except for the occasional direction and the Mireille Mathieu record singing in the background. Neither had even suggested opening wine. Tess had always viewed alcohol as an amplifier of good times, and joy. Drinking when she felt sad just made her feel sadder. And tonight, she certainly felt sad.

Henry broke the silence over dinner. "Well, Tess," was all he could manage.

She held his gaze and let him read her eyes. They could not say what they wanted to say, the truth would have broken the agreement of the weekend. Every second of wordless eye contact further solidified the unspoken knowledge that they had not, in fact, gotten each other out of their systems. Instead, they had so deeply entangled themselves in one another that the agreed-upon end of this timeline would require some truly painful unraveling. Maybe just one more night would soften the blow.

"I'll stay the night and be gone before you wake," she offered.

"And you're sure? This is what you want?" She knew he had to ask the question, but she could not bear to actually answer.

"You've been such a wonderful surprise," she said instead. "And we will be friends. I just...thank you for all of this. For sharing yourself with me. You're just...you're like..."

"A sunbeam?"

She nodded, smiling with her whole body.

The dishes were cleaned. Teeth brushed. Tasks completed, with nothing left but to lay in bed, soaking each other up.

Sex for the final time was slow, methodical, present. It lacked passion and hunger, but the thoroughness implied they both wanted to memorize the other person and the feeling of being together. Henry passed out, clutching Tess as if she were a newborn baby, terrified of her slipping through his fingers.

Tess lay awake for the majority of the night, drifting into short bouts of sleep. She briefly dreamed she was a tree watching her surroundings shift from late fall to early winter. Her leaves died and fell into a crispy blanket on the forest floor, and she stood tall and bare, unprotected. Vulnerable to the elements, knowing the cold was coming.

In the early morning remnants of moonlight, Tess awoke with just enough resolve to untangle her limbs from his. Kissing Henry for the final time on his beautiful, browned shoulder, she collected her clothes, pausing at the door to burn the image of him into her brain. Once it was captured, she slipped out, careful to shut the door softly.

Ancient hardwoods creaked as she tiptoed through his cottage, navigating little scraps of paper strewn across the floor, full of lyrics and musings and words he thought were interesting. What she would give to gather them up and sew them into a dress so she could wear him.

A single tear and a box breath later, she was gone.

Twelve

There was nothing like good, old-fashioned internalized shame to get Tess moving.

She finished the morning in her own bed and awoke hours later with a full mental list of penance for luxuriously indulging in eating and drinking and sex and romance all weekend. That and the distraction she would need from how odd it felt to wake up alone.

She found herself physically shaking her head as the feeling hit her as if she could shake the comfort she had felt with Henry right out of her skin. It lingered like it had become a part of her. He had nestled his way into her mind and body in a way she could not admit to herself. Instead, she would have to work.

The words were flowing that morning, maybe too easily. She found her mind wandering to his fingers. Back to Laozi. *His dimples*. Back to solipsism. *His eyes*. Back to reincarnation. Edgar was going to have a conniption over the roller coaster of these few chapters. At least she would have something substantial for him to critique in their editing meeting, even if it might send him right over the edge.

She committed to thinking less and continued to pour out every other thought she had, skipping over the curves of Henry's back and smell of his cooking and the way he ran his fingers through his hair.

Three thousand words later, Tess allowed herself to take tea in the garden before her meeting with Edgar. The beige mug she pulled from the cupboard sent a pang of missing *her* teacup—the Churchill blue china with a chip by the handle that Henry kept washed and ready for her tea at any moment. Stale toast with jam was a stark contrast to the mouth-watering food she'd had prepared for her all weekend. Nevertheless, she committed to positivity and swung the back door wide to take her tea and toast in solitude in the garden.

There, in the middle of the plants, stood a furious-looking Antoinette. Her scrunched nose and furrowed brow progressively deepened as she examined the tomatoes, muttering to herself. Tess had a split second to decide whether to address her in all her fury, or quietly slip back inside, catching the door so it would not bang shut.

"*Bonjour!* Would you like some tea?" Tess called, as if cheerily greeting Antoinette would diffuse her anger. The sick feeling in her stomach at the fear that someone would be mad at or disappointed in her never quite lessened from her childhood. Presently it spread over her entire body, taking over like a weed.

Although Antoinette had yet to speak, the rate at which she was shaking the tomato in her hand at Tess indicated she was, indeed, in trouble.

"*Fille stupide!*" she finally yelled, confirming Tess's fear. "The tomatoes will die. You say you garden—how you don't know this?"

Tess froze, gripping her tea and toast, unable to conjure up words to soothe Antoinette's anger or even ask for specifics.

"My tomato jam. Is dead. Is all gone—*bonjour, fille?!*"

"I—I'm sorry," Tess muttered, slightly shrugging and shaking her head with confusion.

"*Je ne peux pas te faire confiance! Je dois tout faire moi-même. Je deviens trop vieille pour ça. C'est exaspérant.*" Very few words permeated Tess's understanding. She would have to sit in the maddening discomfort of this until Antoinette could calm down and explain what the hell was going on. Her English seemed to worsen, the madder she got. *In two-three-four, hold two-three-four, out two-three-four, hold two-three-four.*

Tess's self-soothing technique seemed to inspire Antoinette to do the same. After a loud, labored breath she ventured to explain her fury.

"The tomatoes. They have blister beetles. Blister beetles need to be removed immediately so they do not spread. They have spread everywhere. This is why you check the tomatoes every day. But you don't check the tomatoes every day. *Je ne suis pas contente, chérie. Je ne suis pas contente.*" Her head shook steadily back and forth as if it were motorized. Tess desperately wished she could switch it off, save herself from sitting in the deep disappointment she had caused.

She *had* caused it. Although Tess had a knack for absorbing responsibility and fault that did not belong to her—something she was actively working on—she only had herself to blame for this one. Days had gone by wrapped up in Henry's arms, eclipsing her responsibilities to Antoinette and the garden. There was nothing she could do to shimmy her way out of the consequence she faced: deep disappointment from a woman she could not impress even with her shiniest self.

"I did miss a few days of checking. I am so, so sorry. I will do everything I can to fix it." Although the collateral damage here was mere tomatoes, she knew the weight this project held for Antoinette. Her prized tomato jam was her purpose. Tess swore she glimpsed a tear in the corner of Antoinette's eye as she continued slowly shaking her head back and forth and turned to hobble back up the road, leaving Tess with her choices and her guilt and a shit ton of beetles.

Tess remained still, sitting in this feeling she used to run from while holding her now lukewarm tea and toast. Discomfort this intense gripped tight to her neck and shoulder muscles like she was wearing a stress backpack. She breathed, relaxed her shoulders slightly and breathed again, letting the feeling sink into her body so it could pass through. This process was still something she had to consciously practice, so contrary to the suppression of feelings she had practiced for decades.

"Let it go." If Tess's childhood home had had a three-word motto etched on the front door, this would be it. Her mother's well-meaning lesson was to remain grounded, stay true to yourself and not let your circumstances control you. Tess's interpretation, however, was "don't feel". Let nothing affect you, be happy all the time and never crack.

For a deeply feeling kid, this created such a tightly packed little black box of feelings deep inside her, constantly on the brink of bursting. And when it did, it was ugly. Her laid-back, nonchalant façade shattered into millions of pieces, and all the feelings so forcefully suppressed shot through the surface. This typically resulted in complete meltdowns at herself, or even worse, haphazardly misplaced on her family.

A sea of mad, sad, confused, hormonally heightened fury would stream out of Tess and flood the whole house, threatening to drown them all. Her parents and siblings didn't deserve it, but they were required to love her unconditionally, right? Even the punching bag she got her for her sixteenth birthday couldn't handle the brunt of all of Tess's suppressed feelings once they were unleashed.

Every Bible study—and Tess typically attended these at least twice a week—taught her to put Jesus first, others second and herself last. Deny, deny, deny. He is greater than I. Twenty-eight years of solidifying this approach to life and emotions and feelings had given therapist Jenny an annual salary's worth of work to do. Tess developed a borderline unhealthy parasocial relationship with Brené Brown with the amount of time she spent poring over her work in her unlearning.

At this point, several years in, her process typically followed four steps:

1. Recognize the feeling. Name it, specifically, without judgment or categorizing the feeling as good or bad. Just acknowledge that it's there.

2. Feel it in your body. Her mental-physical connection was strong, and she often had visceral reactions to intense emotions through her shoulders and stomach.

3. Breathe through it. Her box breathing practice was still a bit unnatural, but she consistently committed to the effort.

4. Let the feeling wash through you. Sometimes she pictured the feeling written in a cloud and watched it float above her head until it was out of sight. After processing through the first three steps, she repeated her mother's words in her head: "Let it go."

At the current moment, in the middle of step three, her mind latched onto another realization: she was now late for her meeting with Edgar.

Time seemed to speed up as her dinosaur laptop decided to show its age in her haste. The spinning beach ball taunted her. She visualized spiking it off a cliff.

"Come on, come on, come ON," she pleaded with the hunk of metal as if she had any control over the thing. The clock on the screen showed that she was only seven minutes late, but she already knew the face she would be greeted with whenever she was finally able to connect with Edgar. The dread of disappointing another person today seemed to send time tumbling even faster, while her computer booted more slowly.

Now nine minutes late, she was greeted with the exact disappointment she was expecting, though there was a slight comfort in Edgar's familiar face. The stunted processing of her interaction with Antoinette crept up into the corner of her eyes and tears teetered on the edge of unleashing down her cheeks. Edgar seemed to read her, as his frustration with her vanished and was replaced by a look of care.

"I'm so sorry," she began, unclear where she would go with this.

"Tess, are—are you okay?"

This simple question, which seemed to always be asked with an expected answer of "yes, I'm fine" from a familiar, caring person, was too much for the moment. She hadn't even known Edgar for two years, but those specific years had been filled with so much change and searching and dismantling of Tess's life that it had created a significant bond between the two of them. He had quickly become one of her favorite people.

Edgar was in his mid-fifties, Puerto Rican, and married to a sweet man named Jeff. His age difference to Tess had created a pseudo-father-daughter bond, and although their relationship was based in professional courtesy, it was always laced with personal care.

He was tough and would not tiptoe around her feelings in his critiques and intentions to squeeze the very best out of her. Yet his softness, the way he said her name when he was genuinely worried about her, formed a bond that placed him high on the list of people she held most dear.

"I am not good," she finally admitted. "The writing is going okay, but I'm a bit of a mess." His eyes begged elaboration, so Tess unleashed the feelings. She recounted the look on Antoinette's face at her failure to maintain her responsibilities, generalized her weekend with Henry and the hole it had left in her heart, and disclosed the raw loneliness that plagued her here. Edgar nodded along, always tracking, and listened until she got it all out.

His whistling exhale punctuated the end of her monologue. Even through the screen, she could feel his presence. Peace washed through Tess at the relief of giving someone her heavy and having them really feel and carry it with her.

"Sorry—I know we have an actual meeting right now and I'm late anyway. I didn't realize how much I had stored up in me."

"It's okay, *querida*. We knew this could be great for your writing, but difficult for you. Right now I just need you to be okay."

"I know. I will be. I think I just need more human interaction on a regular basis."

"Well that man is just down the road now, isn't he?"

She hoped the pixelated screen was enough to hide the slight blush that covered her cheeks. "I don't know if he's the best person for me to spend my time with right now. But I will schedule more time to talk with friends back home. And if I can ever get back in good graces with Antoinette, maybe I could spend some time with her."

"Maybe. Whoever you need to be near to feel like yourself and work through your stuff before it takes over you works for me," he mused.

Henry. Henry made her feel like herself. He listened, probed for more. He was the closest she had gotten to feeling at home out here. If not for her own goddamn rules.

"Anyway, talk to me about the chapters. You finished all three? I didn't see them come through my email." Shit. Another thing she hadn't done.

"Shoot, yeah, sorry. Coming to you now." The first chunk of chapters *whooshed* across the ocean from Tess's laptop to Edgar in New York. As he pulled up the document, she settled deeper into her chair.

Tess often struggled with what to do while someone was reading her writing. It felt so vulnerable and bare, and she found herself scouring the person's face for any sign of reaction. *Do you like me? Do I sound stupid? Should I give it up now?* As if anticipating rejection before it came would actually soften the blow.

Edgar's notes often followed the sandwich technique: positive feedback, critique(s), positive feedback. Tess tended to hold her breath through the first two categories and could only release when he got to the second bun of the sandwich and she knew she had survived the meat of the critiques.

Although not particularly clear on the screen, Edgar's pleasant facial expression and occasional "mhmm" indicated that he was pleased with her work, sending her fingers out into a fan released from a fist. She had yet to even reread her own writing and had been idea-dumping the whole day.

Something about the weekend she had spent and the conversations she and Henry shared opened a window into her own introspection that allowed her ideas to flow. She couldn't entertain the possibility that spending time with him may not actually be a distraction and could help her writing. The boundary had already been set.

"Well, the writing needs polishing, for sure, but I like where you are going here. It is more *you* than I was expecting. I was prepared to have to strip you of your facts and findings and push you into self-disclosure and vulnerability. But you have done that beautifully so far. Keep that up and I think we really have something here. You'll get my notes by the end of the day tomorrow. I've got to run to my next meeting." This was Edgar being exceptionally kind, as her lateness and emotional dam-breaking had eaten up the bulk of their brief hour together.

"Okay—and sorry again for being late and being a mess. It won't happen again."

"It is good to see your face. I'll be checking in more regularly. Take care of yourself, Tess. Do what you need to do to be a person *and* a writer. Talk soon."

"Thanks for this, really. Talk soon."

Foomp. The sound of her laptop mimicked the mental closing of her day, almost all of which had been shit until Edgar. If ever there was a time to shut down her brain for the day, this was it. Her legs itched to get outside.

Without tracking, and music, and set routes, running had become enjoyable for the first time. Tess found herself feeling the ground beneath her feet. She noticed unique-looking trees, heard the birds, marveled at the clouds. There was no record of how far she ran or how many calories she burned. She simply allowed her body to do what it wanted, what it needed that day. Her pace was all over the place, and she welcomed the desire to switch to walking in the middle of her run. Gone were the days of waking up with a sense of dread that it was a running day. She ran only if and when she wanted to.

This was her fourth run out here in the French countryside, and each unlocked a deeper connection with her legs and her feet and the ground and further broke her chained relationship to discipline and statistics.

A long shower, simple dinner and large glass of wine seemed to be the request of her body post-run, and she happily obliged. Tonight she would sleep, reset, and try again tomorrow.

Thirteen

For four nights straight sleep taunted Tess like a golden medallion, hanging just inches above her but out of reach. Her nights were fitful. Anxiety dreams about Antoinette and writing and Henry and laying at the bottom of the ocean tied to a refrigerator kept her brain buzzing.

She found herself slower to write and less likely to make smart choices to satisfy her physical needs. Her wine supply was quickly draining as her REM cycles shortened.

The bulk of her time had been spent in the garden, hell-bent on restoring good favor with Antoinette. Blister beetles, it turned out, were actual crawling sons-of-bitches and extremely difficult to eradicate. Most times in Tess's life her relentless tenacity was unhelpful and inconvenient. This time it carried her.

She spent hours—too many to count—obsessively plucking and murdering blister beetles. When she was sure she had squashed them all she would see one more, and then three and then ten, in true Sisyphean manner.

Tess squeezed every drop of light out of her days in the garden until she could no longer make out the silhouette of a beetle. Nights were quiet, and she was able to make progress on her reading goals. Loneliness weighed on her, and she wondered if she was purposefully ignoring Edgar's advice to connect with people. After multiple messages from Maria, she finally caved.

"Uh, hi?" Maria seemed to question once their Zoom call connected.

"Hi back?"

"It's just—you look different. Are you okay?"

Sigh. "I'm okay. I am not out-of-this-world fantastic, but I am okay. Everyone wants to know if I'm okay."

"Yeah, I guess people care about you, I don't know. I'm surprised I haven't heard from you in so long."

"It's been busy here. I am doing really well on my writing deadlines. Personally struggling a bit. It's lonely."

"Aren't you like in the middle of nowhere? How are you busy? Tess, *everyone* warned you this was a bad idea and that you'd be lonely and sad and all sorts of bad combinations. I'm not trying to be a dick to you, but it sucks to care about you and watch you make these decisions and then not even respond when you're struggling. Sorry, but you're not busy—I call bullshit."

Tess processed for a minute. This was exactly the conversation she should have expected. She wondered if she subconsciously wanted it, as she had decided to call Maria instead of Jo. Jo would have wholeheartedly supported her, even if she was being stupid and reckless with herself. Maria would call her out. As much as it annoyed her, she must have known she needed it.

"Yeah, dude, I know. I'm just like, mentally busy, I guess. I'm trying to do better."

"Okay. I know it's harsh. I just can't watch you do this to yourself. Do you have any people there?"

"There is a guy down the road." Tess had not planned on relaying this story. The silly embarrassment she felt after gushing to Edgar still clung to her cheeks.

"Tess. I know you," Maria responded, slightly softer. Whether she was caring aggressively or tenderly, she was the most caring person Tess knew. "Tell me whatever you want and don't tell me what you don't want, but obviously there's something."

Tess let the silence hang for a second, not moving in case she needed to claim a screen freeze. Pros and cons of recounting her experience with Henry speed-argued in her head. She finally decided that maybe if she talked about it, she wouldn't think about it so much.

"Yeah, I don't want to make it a huge thing. His name is Henry. He's British and incredibly lovely and sensitive and unfortunately gorgeous. I spent the whole weekend with him, but I can't go down that path. I have so much pressure on me to work on this book. I don't have time for a summer fling,"

Maria's pixelated eyebrow unmistakably raised half an inch. "Well that's...interesting. Not what I was expecting to hear. What do you feel about it?" If only people would stop asking and let her *not* feel so she didn't feel *so* much she might break.

She had no problem not masking her annoyed sigh at Maria. "I like him. I like him a lot. I just don't really know myself in this way. Jake is pretty much the only relationship I've had in my life. I haven't really done casual sex, until now. I don't know if I'm just not capable of it or if this thing with Henry is real. But either way, there's no world in which this becomes an *actual* real thing, and I'd rather not deal with the heartbreak in the meantime. I could use a friend for sure, I just don't know if that's possible with Henry at this point."

"Sounds like you're in deep to me. So like…what would happen if you didn't make so many rules and overanalyze and fear the worst? What would you do?"

She knew the answer to this question, which was the main reason she had made her rules and set her boundaries in the first place. The emotional toll of this conversation had already exhausted her as it always did when she was forced to confront herself. She needed out of this line of questioning. One more shallow, self-unaware answer wouldn't kill her today.

"I don't really know. But I can't really afford to find out."

Tess had ditched her Apple watch for the sake of her simpler French life. Otherwise, she certainly would have gotten an irregular heartbeat alert at the knock that came at the door. The frizzy white halo of Antoinette's head through the window rather than a curly brown mop sent her heart dropping in disappointment.

"The tomatoes look better," Antoinette blurted the second the door cracked wide enough. Tess purposely filled the gap with her body so Antoinette would not see the state of her cottage and dole out another rant of disappointment at her. For now, she wanted to savor the praise for saving the precious tomatoes.

"Thanks. I had to pluck the blister beetles off individually, but everything is looking much better."

"Yes, you did. Don't let a problem like that get out of hand again." Curt, correct and applicable to several aspects of Tess's life. "Come to the main house for dinner tomorrow night. You are lonely."

"Oh, thanks so much, but I'm alright on my own," Tess lied, lacking the social energy required to have dinner again with a near-stranger who seemed to think she was kind of worthless.

"You will come and bring a basket of tomatoes. I need peppers, rosemary, basil. You will bring and I will cook for you."

Tess's chin bounced above her chest in subconscious obedience before her brain could process.

"A *nice* dinner, *à six heures*," Antoinette added before turning to leave as abruptly as she'd come. She paused and squinted up at the sky as if searching for UFOs, muttering to herself in French. Her straw hat sat so far back on her head that it appeared to hang on a single hair.

"Thank you, *au revoir!*" Tess shouted after her. Antoinette snapped back into the moment and nodded sharply at her before resuming hobbling back up the road with her slight limp.

The invitation loomed over Tess like an unwanted hand on her shoulder she couldn't quite shake off. Her previously ambiverted tendencies seemed to have shifted completely to the introvert side, and the idea of this dinner sat uncomfortably heavy in her future plans.

The distance her heart rate had traveled between the initial knock and the unwanted dinner date sucked all her mental energy. Back to her hands she went.

A lump of yellow linen fabric sitting on the chair next to her sewing machine had been taunting her all week. The light, airy sundress she had initially envisioned had taken a turn toward impossible as she had already sewn and ripped and re-sewn the bodice twice now. Antoinette's invitation reinvigorated her vision for the pile, as she seemed to need to prove to herself that she could do hard things. With her mental gas gauge on empty, she tapped over into her body and let her hands fly.

Linen was a favorite for Tess, as its soft but scratchy texture always felt right. The fabric didn't pretend to be something it wasn't. It wrinkled. Hard. And stayed wrinkled. Like it was allowed to be imperfect—a state Tess longed to embody herself. It always felt light yet comforting on her body. Stable. The fabric itself was easy to work with because of its sturdy nature, and it tended to hold a stitch exactly where it was placed without stretch.

As she rounded the final curve of the bodice, she let out a deep sigh. Sewing held such a stark juxtaposition of satisfaction for completing a task and dissatisfaction with the result needing a complete overhaul. Finishing and undoing and starting again.

The bodice fit more loosely than the flattering sundress Tess had imagined, but the flowy skirt felt perfect. Her tanned skin worked with the yellow in a way her mother had always warned never would, keeping her in muted grays and blacks much of her life. Yellow quite suited Tess as a visual of what her soul felt like, and in the summer it just worked. She would wear it the next night solely to please herself, not expecting a word from Antoinette about the ensemble.

———

The late-August sun beat hot the next afternoon and Tess regretted that she had not picked the vegetables and herbs sooner in the day. At this rate she'd have no time to bathe before the "nice dinner," and her flowy handmade yellow dress would have to serve as her sole effort in looking presentable. Her hair was unsalvageable at this point and would have to be shoved up in a bun, slightly damp with sweat. Even still, she was on track to be late to the nice dinner where she was providing the bulk of the food.

Some quick snips at the rosemary bushes completed her harvesting task, taking advantage of every inch her basket could hold. She jogged into the house to change, run a washcloth over her face and throw her hair up, before tackling the task of transporting the basket as she rode her bike up the road to the main house.

Tess glanced down the path to check for signs of Henry before taking off—struck with both relief and disappointment when she didn't see him. Pushing off easily, she breezed up the road with her load more swiftly than she'd expected. Her long days in the garden and rekindled running routine had toned and increased the muscle mass in her whole body.

Her smirk turned to a full-on grin as she thought of how far she had come since the day she struggled to ride home with her treasures from Didier's. Tangible progress was addicting.

When she arrived, a loud, squawking laugh coming from the terrace had Tess do a double take at the entrance to be sure she was in the right place. To be fair she had never heard Antoinette laugh before, but it seemed almost impossible that a sound like that would come from a woman like her. Intrigued, she ducked through the open doorway, following the laughter down the hall, through the kitchen and out to the terrace.

As Tess stepped out the back door, the view over the vineyard that had stopped her in her tracks on her last visit barely registered in her brain. All the blood drained from her face as she was instead struck by the sight of the back of a head of brown, curly hair.

Antoinette's eyes met hers and Tess caught the slight lift of her eyebrow. She knew. Tess scrambled to wipe the "I spent a weekend next to, on top of and underneath this man" look off her face.

"*Bonsoir*, Tess. You've met Henri, yes?" Not really a question.

As Henry stood and turned and locked eyes with her, Tess nearly stumbled backward at the impact. For the last week, she had done everything in her power to minimize, rationalize and bring herself down to earth from the heaven of that weekend. But here he was, in the flesh. Undeniably Tess's heaven on earth.

"*Bonsoir*, Tess," Henry replied coolly as he kissed both of her cheeks. He seemed significantly less surprised to see her than she was to see him, and she couldn't help but hope that the invite had been his doing in an effort to see her. Either way, here they were. Strapping in for the long haul of an hours-long French dinner.

Antoinette's eyes darted back and forth between the pair who could not take their eyes off each other. Tess awkwardly thrust the basket of vegetables and herbs toward Antoinette.

"I brought the—"

"*Oui, je vois*," Antoinette interjected, giving voice to her annoyance over her intrigue. "I cook, so you two...look," she muttered as she walked off. This was certainly not the night Tess had envisioned for herself, and mentally threw away all her prepared conversation topics.

Henry sat back down and took a large swig of his wine before reaching over to pour Tess's glass. She took the seat beside him, as Antoinette's glass occupied the place across.

"Thanks. I didn't know you would be here."

"I did," he confirmed. So that settled that.

"Well, it's good to see you."

"It is...good to see you too." The corners of his mouth twitched as if he were suppressing a smile. "Your dress suits you. I'm glad you finished it." She could not suppress her own smile. He looked good. A necklace of pearls hung above his linen button-down, the Henry version of "nice dinner" attire.

"It's different than I meant it to be, but I've decided I like it."

"You'll have to make me one next."

"You need a dress? Going on a fancy date or something?"

"Nah, my dating life hasn't exactly gone to plan. I just want something pretty to garden in so I can feel lovely too," he said, fake flicking hair off his shoulder. As if he could be lovelier.

"Mmm, well I'll get right on that," she mused.

The sun had started setting over the horizon of the garden so spectacularly as if it knew it needed to compete with their view of each other. They sat silently, mesmerized, as the wine started to settle into Tess's body and smooth out jagged lines of stress and fear and tension. It made its way to her feet, strongly connecting her to the ground. She continued to sip and let the wine settle deeper into her as she settled deeper into the moment.

"How has the writing been coming then?" Henry asked, holding his gaze at the sunset.

"Pretty well, actually. I fucked up Antoinette's tomatoes, so I spent much of the week plucking blister beetles off them. But I've had this surge of writing streaks that are adding up fairly well. My agent is pleased."

"Sounds like you've been inspired. By blister beetles, maybe."

"Hah. Maybe. Any new songs?"

"A few, actually. Turns out I've been pretty inspired myself."

"I can't wait to hear them—" she blurted, honestly, without thinking.

"Well, I'm sure that could be arranged..."

Antoinette's shrill whistle pulled them out of the conversation so Tess could avoid having to respond to the offer. Another reminder that their agreement, the distance she put between their two cottages, was totally up to her.

"I need one of you. Just one. The one who can cook," Antoinette called to them, obviously requesting Henry over Tess.

"At your service!" he called back, scrambling to get up and jog over to her as quickly as possible. Antoinette's loud laugh bellowed again into the wide-open air.

Dinner was smoother than Tess would have imagined, having stumbled upon such a different energy than she had expected that night with the addition of Henry. He carried much of the conversation and continued to get Antoinette rolling with laughter. She seemed so much more at ease than Tess had experienced her, and it became clear that the Henry effect could work on anyone. He even bridged the gap between the two women, something Tess had worried she might never mend after the tomato fiasco.

The food really was very good, and there was certainly no shortage of wine. Each sip gave Tess another slight release of tension until she found herself totally relaxed and sinking in her seat. The rosy haze of the sunset through the filter of several glasses of wine gave the night a picturesque, romantic hue. Every time Henry caught her eye, warmth spread throughout her body.

Antoinette made several small knowing comments about the two of them that Henry countered with witty diversions. Tess couldn't quite get a clear reading on whether Antoinette seemed to approve of a romantic connection, or if she was too protective over Henry to ship a short-term fling with a soft-hearted American tomato murderer.

"I'm off to bed," Antoinette inserted abruptly, significantly earlier than Tess had imagined the night would go. They had finished dinner and almost two bottles of wine, but she had anticipated dessert and coffee and lounging until the sky was black.

"I'm old. It's time," Antoinette added after noticing the slightly confused looks on her guests' faces.

"We'll carry this in. You go ahead. Thanks for such a lovely evening. You never cease to amaze me, you majestic woman," Henry crooned. How was Tess supposed to follow up a compliment like that?

"It really was fantastic. Thank you so much for having us!" Tess found her volume increasing as Antoinette had already begun hobbling off to bed, waving an arm back at her as if to say, "You're welcome."

The pair cleared the table and washed the dishes amid flirty exchanges. Henry's hand began lingering longer on the small of her back as he passed behind her, and the touch of their fingers when handing off dishes became more electrifying. Tess was reminded of how comfortable and easy it felt to work together, like they had been a partnership for years with a couple's routine down pat.

"Walk me home?" he asked when they were done, cheeky as ever.

"I rode here."

"Walk me home while I walk your bike home?"

Despite knowing the extent to which this would stretch her self-control and adherence to her own rules, she obliged. In turn, his smile stretched so wide it seemed to reach for his ears.

The night had unfolded so magically and their connection so undeniably that Tess imagined there was no way he would not address it. Why else would he have pushed to walk with her? He had hinted and flirted and winked all night—he had to know it too.

She mentally braced herself the entire walk, preparing to shut him down and remind him of their agreement and what was at stake. If she didn't have her guard up, her heart would take over and respond with her actual desires.

Instead, he whistled, and kicked rocks, and mused at the stars the entire walk home. Finally, at her walkway, he turned to face her head-on, standing just an inch too close to hide his intentions.

"Well, you've been quiet. Anything you'd like to say to me?"

Of course he would just ask outright. And, of course, Tess was not prepared for this type of direct communication.

"I...we just..." she stuttered before mirroring his deep breath. "It's just really good to see you."

"It's really good to see you, Tess." He was quite serious now, lacking his usual cheeky undertone. His eyes searched hers, seeking the answers to his questions.

Yes, this is real. So goddamn real that I don't know how to be around you. But I want to.

He seemed to read her like a book. She broke his gaze before she gave it all away, but it felt like she had already revealed the truth: that if they went their separate ways tonight, she might just break. All this self-awareness and truth-telling and knowing herself made it very difficult for Tess to control the situation.

Eventually he nodded, turned on his heel and strode off. When he had passed the trees, she swore she heard him singing the melody they had sung together that day, riding bikes in unison. "*Dada da da, da-dada da da.*"

She remained at the edge of the walkway until she could no longer see or hear any sign of him, soaking up as much of him as she could.

Fourteen

Tess woke up the next morning with the same familiar lie that used to run through her hungover head in her early twenties when the biblical rule book finally allowed alcohol: *I am never drinking again.*

I am never seeing him again.

The Henry Hangover felt just as physical as it did emotional. Her body weighed heavy on her mattress, like she wasn't sure if she could lift herself up or if she would fall right out of bed. The space he was now occupying in her head was so expansive she could barely find a way to connect her brain to her body to tell it to get up. For better or worse, whether she wanted it or not, he had taken over.

She finally flung her heavy legs over the side of the bed and shuffled out to her typewriter to try emptying her brain to make space for literally anything else.

Henry.

His eyes are the sky.

His smile is the earth.
I want to dig a hole and curl up in it.
A shallow grave.
What the fuck am I doing.

The stacks of paper that held her daily typewriting read like a playbook for slipping steadily into insanity. There were no usable poems, little introspection and bad writing.

Even so, she had a lifetime of anecdotal evidence of what happened when she didn't write, when she couldn't attribute words to the waves of emotion that flowed through her. So, even if her mind had not even an inch of space for a creative thought, she would write.

When she was stuck, she had to remove herself from the keys and reset her mind. Getting dressed was one of her daily morning goals so as not to stay in an oversized Reputation Tour T-shirt all day every day. This morning her shorts slid up less gracefully, hugging her body tighter than before. She marveled at the imprint this country had left on her, filling her out with baguettes and muscle and wine.

There was a time in Tess's life when she would have burst into tears at her shorts catching on extra belly that seemed to have not been present the previous day. As she ran her hand across her soft abdomen she smiled, grateful for the ability to love herself within change that she previously had felt was impossible.

"Welp. More me to love," she said aloud. "What a joy." An idea sparked as she clamored back to her typewriter.

What a joy

To
Wake up with
Five more pounds
Connecting me to the ground
Taking up more space
Strengthening my resolve
Against the gravity to hold me down
What a joy
To
Choose not to hate that
There is more of me
To love and be loved
To choose what
I want to do
Who I want to be with more of me
What a joy
To
Laugh at a scale
As if it had the power
To measure all that I am
What I hold
In my body and my mind—

A loud melodic sound outside caused Tess's head to shoot up, like the prairie dogs she had seen at the zoo in the fourth grade. Silence followed. At this point, her gut reaction was to worry that she was starting to hear things and solitude had pushed her over the line into some sort of psychotic break. She shook her head and returned her fingers to the keys.

This sacred home—

Another sound, unmistakably a guitar this time, froze her in place. She would not let her heart run faster than her mind but couldn't imagine where else a guitar sound might be coming from. Reckoning with reality, she realized someone was indeed playing music outside her cottage.

Tess slowly tiptoed toward the front door, as if she was afraid of scaring the person away, still in her oversized T-shirt and socks. The slowness with which she was moving, more honestly, came from her own fear. She wanted it to be him, and if she opened the door and it wasn't, her heart threatened to fall right out of her chest.

Finally, she reached the door, just in time to hear the beginning of the vocals to the song. The familiar "*dada da da, da dada da da*" settled into her ears and she flung the door open to confirm that Henry was at the edge of the garden. Singing. To *her*.

Tess had been serenaded once before. In high school, a boy named Tim commandeered a youth group worship session to profess his feelings for her. He had been playing guitar for the group around the fire but asked everyone to just listen as he turned to her. The result was a painfully uncomfortable worship song about loving God that he instead sang at Tess—something she had certainly not expected and deeply wanted to end as soon as possible. The memory of discomfort as she sat there, awkwardly smiling but not sure where to look, mentally pleading for it to end, was still palpable. When it was over, she side-hugged Tim, left the worship night, and never answered his texts again.

The scene before her now conjured a completely different reaction. She found her eyes locked into Henry's without the slightest whiff of discomfort. He sang *to* her instead of at her, as if he had written the song just for her. The lyrics built a picture of a woman shining so bright he almost had to look away but couldn't, crescendoing into a chorus plainly written about her:

"*You're my sunbeam,*" he sang over and over, as the words seared deeper into her. She leaned against the doorframe to stabilize herself, not even blinking for fear of missing any part of this moment.

The song carried on. It was beautiful—the boy could surely sing. The lyrics felt whimsical and fun, putting words to how she felt in her yellow linen dress. Like how she wanted to be seen. He finished with their shared melody, and she joined in.

Henry's mouth broke into a giant singing smile that she gladly matched.

"*Dada da da, da dada da da, dada da da, da dada da da,*" they sang together, smiling at each other in mutual understanding, ending at the same time.

"You said you wanted to hear what I've been working on!" he called to her as if he needed an explanation for being there.

They held their goofy smiles for a minute before Tess's body caved. In seconds she was up against him, running her hands through his curly brown hair, kissing his face all over. Touching like this again after a week apart shook Tess so deeply her knees threatened to buckle underneath her. He held on to her tightly, alternating her kisses with his until their lips found each other. Tess stepped backward into her cottage, bringing him with her without separating.

Minutes or hours later—Tess wasn't sure and certainly didn't care, they lay tangled up in her bed, hands deep in each other's hair. Her fingers grasped a tuft at the nape of his neck. The position was comfortable, safe, as if she belonged there. Like she had been away for the past week, and now she was home.

"Susceptible to wooing. Noted," he finally said with his cheeky smile. She hugged him more tightly.

"I was teetering so close to the edge of giving in. I think if you showed up offering me a bouquet of freshly sharpened pencils I would have caved. I will say you put on a good show."

"I wrote that song in my head in the garden with you. I didn't mean to disrespect your boundaries. I just thought maybe you should hear it."

"Fuck my boundaries. I don't know what I'm doing. I was drowning in you not being around. You have no idea how badly I needed you to show up today."

He stroked her back, staring up at the ceiling.

"And you *had* to know this would be the result," she quipped.

Minutes later, he murmured softly into her hair. "I hoped. I don't know what I'm doing either. I don't want to hurt you."

The comment, said so many times by so many people with varying degrees of awareness, held palpable weight here. It recognized, firstly, that this *was* real. They could not deny it, and it would only become more real with time. And secondly, that this *would* end. There was no future for them outside of this estate. They would inevitably hurt each other.

As Tess knew all too well, the more stitches you run connecting two pieces of fabric, the harder and more painful it is to rip them apart. Looking up into Henry's eyes, she let go, stomping on the metaphorical foot pedal, fusing them so tightly she couldn't imagine how they would ever be separated.

September

Fifteen

Cue the rom-com montage of early relationship bliss.

They spent the majority of their time at Henry's cottage and in the garden. Tess's cottage existed only for calls to Edgar and Jo and Maria because of its slightly less terrible Wi-Fi. She would tread back to take her calls, fully intending on staying there for a while to be alone. Every time, sooner than she'd planned, she'd find reasons of varying legitimacy to need to head back to him.

Eventually, she lugged her typewriter and sewing machine to their new home in his study. Together they hung her painting above his fireplace as if to mark the space as their home. Each morning, they sipped Earl Grey from their matching Churchill china teacups.

The natural cadence of their coexistence happened more comfortably than Tess's marriage experience. They were together, physically near each other, almost always. Sometimes they were truly, intentionally together, but often they parallel-played along in their individual lives.

She wrote. He wrote. She sewed; he sang. They danced a lot and laughed even more. The ease with which this arrangement worked itself out surprised Tess. She loved to be with him, wanted to be near him and cherished her alone time. Like two rivers flowing together—splitting off, winding back—they morphed their individual French countryside summers into one united fall.

It was all there. The intellectual and emotional depth, the lighthearted silliness, the passionate romance. In this bubble, they were perfectly matched. Although their world was small and fragile with a set expiration date, it held temporary safety.

Weekly dinners at Antoinette's became a routine. The actuality of their relationship was never spoken about but quietly accepted. Didier occasionally joined and stole the show every time, chain-smoking and making lewd comments in French for Antoinette's enjoyment. These people in this place were becoming etched on Tess's soul with precious, fond memories she knew would become permanent.

If she really counted it up, Tess doubted she had had as much sex with Jake in seven years as she did with Henry in mere weeks. Honestly, her sex life with Jake had been incredibly bleak. Physical connection with Henry was off the charts. With the removal of shame and self-denial, she was able to experience true physical desire, and she had plenty of it to keep them busy.

The most confusing part about sex in Christianity is that you aren't allowed to think about it or do it before you're married, and then some magical switch is supposed to flip on your wedding night. Tess remembered lying with Jake, feeling like her switch was broken. It didn't feel like the worshipful, giving of herself to her husband she had been promised by older women. It was disappointing, laughably quick and impossible to separate from the shame she had been trained to associate with sexuality.

With Henry, she didn't feel like she was giving herself to him. It felt more like he admired her, and she admired him back. Even after sex they would lay and stare at each other for too long, running their hands up and down each other's bodies. He was really the most beautiful man she had ever encountered.

Henry lived so unapologetically himself, so unconcerned with rules and boxes and expectations. The plane of his life was such a wide-open field that he could go in any direction, spin around, head backward. Tess was on a contact high, breathing in his intoxicating tranquility and lightheartedness and letting it take form in her. She began to know him, truer and deeper than she knew most people. With each new level, she wanted more and allowed him to venture just as far into her own self with ease.

"What's the worst thing you've ever done?" he asked over dinner one night, reaching for a deeper intimacy.

Tess sighed, mentally thumbing through her Rolodex of quirky anecdotes, searching for the best, not-so-bad answer, and landed in high school.

"When I was in tenth grade my friend Annie and I were in Biology. We hated it. We're both terrible at science and our teacher always had to separate us because we couldn't stop talking. I was used to getting good grades in most classes but was doing really poorly—which I would love to blame on Annie. In all honesty, we didn't listen, messed around during labs and had no notes to study from.

"Anyway, one day we walked into class to find graded tests on our desks. Annie got an eight out of a hundred, and I got a twelve. We were both immediately furious at our teacher and way too immature to recognize it was only our own fault. Ms. Simon wasn't in the room, but her favorite Johnny Cash CD was playing in this little blue boombox at the back of the class. No one else was in class yet, so without really thinking we took the CD out of the boombox and tossed it out the window." Tess paused and winced, glancing sideways at his reaction. "Ms. Simon was so upset when she came back into the class and kept asking us if we knew anything about what happened to it. We just lied over and over, which I hate and suck at. We never owned up to it and Annie and I never even talked about it again. Ugh, it grosses me out to think about it. It was so out of character for me. I wonder what ever happened to poor Ms. Simon."

"How do you mean 'out-of-character'?" he asked, brow furrowed, processing.

"I just mean I was a good kid. I followed rules and respected everyone, especially teachers. My mom would be horrified if she knew I did that."

"So you were good, and you did something bad."

Tess paused. There she was, trying to shove herself back into a box. The right box! The "good" box. How could she *be* good and *do* something so bad? And there he was, lovingly pointing out the nuances of good and bad, dismantling the boxes altogether. Making more space for Tess to just be Tess.

He watched her process and let it lie.

"Did you at least fail Biology?" he asked, half smiling.

"Not even. I got up to a B."

"So you never got your punishment."

"Only the punishment I inflict on myself. I haven't thought about that story in a long time. I'd rather not remember myself in that light."

"Yeah, a CD stealer. What a monster."

"Obviously it's your turn now. Give it to me."

Henry twirled his pasta entirely too many times so that the bite would never have fit in his mouth. He slid his fork out and started this process two more times, clearly stalling. Tess waited.

He met her eyes, put his fork down and sighed.

"I destroyed a marriage," he said, stone-faced, adding a nonchalant shrug. She let him search her eyes for judgment and refused to give it to him.

"Tell me more. I want all of it," Tess said, matching his gaze.

"After Celine, I was a wreck. I had a distorted view of myself after a little bit of fame, and I became such an asshole. I was mostly just very selfish in a way that doesn't feel like it fits who I'm made to be.

"Anyway, I had a tour manager named Nadine. She was about fifteen years older than me and gorgeous, strong, really sure of herself. Married with two kids. I was taken with her from the beginning, but somewhere along the tour, I decided I was going to do something about it. I went after her, hard. I was still sleeping with other women almost every night but threw all my efforts at her. She denied me for quite a while until she didn't.

"After the first time we slept together she made me promise this would be it. I could barely look her in the eyes after. It felt like I drained her of her power and her poise and replaced it with shame." He paused again, knowing by now that Tess would give him full room to finish.

"It didn't stop there, of course. I was obsessed. She tried to end it so many times, but I wouldn't let her. I threatened to tell her husband. I loved her for sure, but it was about something more than that. Power, maybe? She was so powerful when I met her, and I was hungry for it. But I just ended up sucking the life out of her.

"Her husband found out. She left the tour and me and her husband. Everyone knew, and some tabloids even picked it up. I was very unprepared for that. It was like I wanted the power and the recognition, but only for the parts of me I wanted everybody to see. When my image tanked, I spiraled even harder. I was doing ecstasy a lot, desperate not to feel. Davey, my drummer, got the band to sit me down and tell me they were going to quit if I didn't figure my shit out and get sober. That was the night I ended up in the field. From there I went to rehab, and now I'm here." He let out such a guttural sigh, Tess felt her own lungs deflate to nothing.

"So that is the worst thing I ever did. Or things, rather. Unless you'd like to hear more."

Tess took her time.

"I'm mostly interested in the way you told that story," she finally responded.

"What do you mean?"

"You had this fire in your eyes as you spoke. It felt like a challenge. Like you're trying to get a reaction out of me or scare me off. Like you think you're too dark and damaged and I can't take it."

It was Henry's turn to pause, letting words turn over in his mind. "I guess that is a fair analysis. Did it work?"

Tess steadily shook her head, mouth curling into a smile. "Not on me."

"Ah. Well. We'll crack on, I suppose," he said, as if this were a test they had passed, and they were now clear for takeoff.

She meant it, truly, that this did not scare her. It matched what she had pictured from his vague references to his first tour experiences anyway. The slight burning in her chest came from her own guilt. He had laid his worst out on the table, expecting her to run, or at least slightly retreat. She hadn't and wouldn't, but she could not help but feel a pang of regret at not matching his vulnerability.

Tess would always see the best in a person, just not herself. And she couldn't bear the thought of her light dimming in his eyes if he also knew her worst. For now, this would have to be the extent to which she let him in.

Weekly video chatting dates with Maria and Jo had become routine. They had each heard rumblings of Henry at this point, but neither were fully briefed on the whole situation. Calls always happened back at her own cottage, away from him. Tess just couldn't bring herself to admit to her friends that she was actually living with this person. Their bubble did not have room for others to be fully pulled in.

Today's call was especially exciting, as Maria had gone up to Portland to be with Jo for their shared birthdays. Tess hopped on ten minutes early, anxiously waiting to see her people together.

"*CHIENNE!!!!!*" they yelled in drunken unison as soon as the call connected. It was early there, but unlike Tess, Maria and Jo could throw back drinks as easily now as they did ten years ago.

"You did *not* learn the French word for bitch."

"Hell yes we did, biiiiiiitch!!"

"Happy birthday you idiots."

"We did something crazy, and you can NOT be mad because it is our birthdays."

"I absolutely can and will be mad if I need to. What did you do."

They giggled for a full minute as Tess rolled her eyes, desperately wishing she was there to be an idiot with them.

"WHAT did you do??"

"We booked a vacation!! In two weeks. Want to guess where we're going?"

Without a second to process, they both yelled, "France, *chienne*!!"

Tess's eyes bulged, mouth dropped open as she scrambled to fix her face.

"Are you just dying? Can you believe anyone could be such an amazing friend?" Jo asked, half kidding and half hopeful.

"I told you she'd be mad," Maria muttered.

"I'm not mad. I'm processing. This is insane. Are you sure? I mean—I would just love to see you guys!" Tess finally managed, truthfully. These were her people, deeply woven into the foundation of her identity. She ached for familiar faces.

She also knew that this would effectively burst the carefully crafted bubble she and Henry had created here in Abzac.

Back from a shopping trip to replenish their refrigerator, Henry and Tess found it hard to get into the groove of work for the day.

Henry lay flat on the ground, staring at the ceiling. He would do this for hours if there were no interruptions. Tess yearned to bring him back down to her. She craved his depth, wanting to venture into the deepest parts of his emotional psyche and soak up all his goodness. Plus, she was over pretending to write while she watched him.

"What is your favorite feeling to feel?"

He ran his thumb along his jawline, seriously pondering the answer. She had to admit she loved this about him, that he trusted her enough to want her to know him deeply. The first answer that came to his head wouldn't suffice—he wanted to dig deep to reveal the truest answer to any question. He was more committed to intimacy with her than she had ever experienced in a relationship.

"Awe," he finally responded, with a noticeable spark in his eyes. "I remember the first time I really felt it, or at least the first time I remember feeling it. I was about twelve watching a sunrise with my Aunt Rita one morning in Halifax. It sounds corny, I know, but I distinctly remember the feeling of watching the sun come up over the Atlantic, drinking my tea wrapped up in a blanket with my favorite person in the world. It felt like life couldn't possibly be this good. Still gets me, honestly," he said, and clearly meant it. "I've chased that feeling though, and it's one of those things you can't make happen for yourself. Like if you expect or seek awe, you'll never get it. It has to be unexpected, where everything is so surprisingly intense that your brain can barely keep up." He smiled at the ceiling, reflecting on the feeling.

"You know, I felt it running with you in the rain that first day. The energy in my body was so charged I thought I'd send out an electric shock if I touched something. At least that's what awe feels like to me."

Tess briefly reminisced on that same feeling, that their meeting was so electric she almost expected to see bolts of energy connecting them. For now, she would archive the comment that she inspired his favorite feeling in the world, and instead head deeper into his beautiful mind.

"Tell me why your Aunt Rita is your favorite person in the world."

"Ooof." He sat up and faced her, dimples fully exposed. Clearly, she'd piqued his interest enough to bring him out of his ceiling contemplation. "That's a tough one to explain. Part of it is who she is, just magnetic and kind and interesting. Part of it is that I spent a lot of time with her growing up.

"My older sister Clara has a rare autoimmune disease. There were so many doctor's appointments and tests and periods where she wasn't doing well, so sometimes my parents sent me to stay with Aunt Rita in Nova Scotia. I always felt a bit guilty for not being there for Clara, but it just seemed like I was in the way. Aunt Rita's house was heaven.

"She would take care of me, like really take care of me, and I got to be a kid in a way I couldn't at home. She never had kids and I feel like she viewed me as hers a bit. But she treated me like a person, someone she really wanted to be around and talk to. We cooked together and played games and explored. The most magical memories of my childhood are with Aunt Rita in Halifax."

Tess had, of course, no knowledge of where Halifax was, and would keep to herself the fact that Nova Scotia being a real place was actually news to her. She made a mental note to look it up later.

"I think that's why I am so connected to Antoinette as well," he continued. "She and Rita grew up together and have a lot of similarities. I find myself drawn to strong, grounded, independent women," he added as he side-glanced at Tess while sipping his tea.

"She sounds incredible. I'm sorry about your sister. That must have made your childhood…tricky." Tess often fumbled her words when she wanted someone to know she saw and understood them, without sounding like she knew exactly what it would be like to have experienced the same thing.

"Tricky," he repeated, seeming to mull over the word and try it out to see if it fit what he felt. "I guess so. I love my sister dearly. She's a good bit older than me, and we didn't get a lot of time to really grow up together. I'm grateful for the ways I became quite independent since my parents weren't always available to parent me. I don't resent it, but I do wish I had more time with them. Sometimes I feel guilty for how much I adore Aunt Rita and make time to talk to and see her when I don't always do the same for my own parents. But yes, it has been tricky at times. Although I believe that's how family is for most people."

This was a topic she had purposely avoided because of her own…tricky situation. Tess had such complicated feelings about her family and was currently in such a bitter stage of her relationship with them that she wasn't sure she wanted to talk about it. She knew he would respect it if she didn't, but also that he wouldn't accept her bullshit answers if she tried to package the situation in a pretty bow, neglecting to divulge the tightly wound knots of pain and love she felt.

"Tricky," she repeated, uncertain of where she was headed with this.

"You don't have to talk about it if you don't want to," he offered, reading her.

"I know. That's the problem, though. I can't just say a little bit to you without saying all of it to you. I can't make it sound not so bad or pretend like I don't feel the way I feel. I can feel you seeing through it on my face if I am not fully disclosing complete honesty."

"Ha!" he laughed, startling her. "That's true. You don't *have* to tell me anything. But if you do, it better be the truth, the whole truth and nothing but the truth. I can't help it; my bullshit detector is too strong. And I'm not just interested in the pretty bits of you, although there are many. I want to know you, and if you don't give me the real you, I don't know you at all."

"I know, and I want you to know me. It's just hard to explain," she began, absentmindedly twirling a curl. "I guess I feel a little protective of them. I love my family and I know they love me, but I don't particularly like them, and I don't think they like who I am at all. Which is...tricky." Her finger throbbed under the pressure of a curl twirled so tight it was cutting off circulation. She released it and pressed on.

"They were devastated when I abandoned my faith. They did and said some really horrible things they thought were right but just about destroyed me. There's a lot about who they are and the way I was raised that I'm grateful for. There's a lot that I struggle with. But at this point, the relationships are so strained that I don't know if they could ever be repaired. Which I'm learning to be okay with, even though it hurts."

There. That was about as honest as she could be about the situation.

He nodded, knowingly, seemingly understanding from his own experiences.

"I still talk to my brother, Luke, sometimes. But after my book and the breakup with Jake, my family was so upset. My little sister Rachel hasn't spoken to me in a year. I haven't had more than a two-minute voicemail interaction with my parents in months.

"To them, what I wrote in my book was poison. They feel like something corrupted my brain to make me question all the things they feel are obviously true and good in the world. I can't explain to them how important it is for me to question, to find my own truth, that just accepting whatever they or some pastor told me isn't true belief. And now they feel like I've thrown poison into the world with my questions. My mom gave me this insane lecture about how I am responsible for what I put out there, and that people are going to get hurt because of me. That cut me so deeply. So, Luke is all I have left of them, and even with him I'm pretty guarded. Trust me—all this is easier to say after having processed it in therapy for the last year. It's tricky and painful and sentimental all at once."

"Wow."

"Yeah."

"Your mom is wrong, of course."

"I think so. I know it all hurt Rachel since she looked up to me, and I can't change that. I do feel proud and hopeful that what I put out into the world will help people rather than hurt people. I also hold great responsibility for it."

"How would encouraging people to seek their own truth hurt them?"

She pondered this one for a second, finding it nearly impossible to explain this to someone who had never relied on something like religion to explain life.

"People find a lot of comfort in religion, social norms and the way things just are. When you pull that rug out, things can really crumble. You pull out the cornerstone and the whole house comes tumbling down. It's a scary place to be when you don't really know what you believe, and you don't have answers."

"I get that—but it sounds scarier to me to accept the answers someone else has given you."

"That's because you're you. You're the youest you I've ever met, the freest bird soaring in your own wind." This was, without question, the cheesiest line Tess had ever uttered out loud. She promptly kissed him to hide her cringe.

He released the kiss, unwilling to let her hide. "Everyone deserves that. And I have to believe that for some people, you've given that to them."

"I hope so."

He grabbed a scrap of lined paper and wrote a word, holding it up for consideration.

"I like the word cornerstone. You should consider that for your new book title."

He was right. Tess knew it. The word held weight, gave a visual. The religious undertones made it a perfect sequel.

"I just might." She winked, grabbing the scrap and tucking it in her pocket. *Cornerstone.*

Sixteen

"Do you have a bathing suit? Or at least bottoms?"

"Huh? Yeah, I mean why?" Tess asked, mind yanked out of the clouds.

"Let's go."

"To the lake?"

"No, I mean let's go. Away. This weekend. *À la plage*. We've stayed within a four-kilometer radius for a month now. I'm aching for a change of scenery, although I'd like to keep you in my view." Henry slid his arm around her waist and pulled her in close. "I want you in the real world. Or at least off this estate. I want to walk around and hold your hand and sip cocktails at the beach. What do you say?"

Every dream Tess had had about the two of them outside of this place was just that—a dream. There was no reality outside of the narrow radius their bikes had taken them. Something about the prospect of taking their romance on the road tensed Tess, as if she wasn't ready to face the music yet. Leaving here meant testing themselves out in the world, and she wasn't sure she wanted to find out if they would pass. On the other hand, a beach trip away with him sounded nearly impossible to pass up.

He sensed her hesitation.

"Look, we can sit around here and do what we've been doing for weeks. Or we can try something and have fun. What's the worst that could happen?"

The boat would be rocked. The bubble would pop. Life and people and circumstances would break their fragile agreement.

"I want to, I just don't know if it's the best idea."

"It's up to you. I'm going, and I hope you come too, *chérie*," he said, tightening his arms around her. She breathed him in and laughed, landing where they both knew she would.

"Ah! Yes. Okay, yes. For fun."

"Brilliant," he breathed, finally kissing her. "I'll book it all."

"Then you must leave me be today. I have loads of writing to do."

"Of course, *madame*. I'll bring you a tea and a scone and be out of your way." He winked, finally releasing her and sauntering off into the kitchen.

Tess sat down at her computer and stared at her notes. Words seemed to swim on the screen, and she often had trouble starting to write until one of them jumped out at her and sparked some creativity. Finally, the word "respect" got her going.

Less than a hundred words into her idea Henry was behind her, rubbing her shoulders after setting down her tea. She lightly shrugged him off, trying to grasp the tail end of the idea before it escaped her.

"Okay, no massage today," he said, kissing her cheek as he pulled a chair up next to her. "What belief are you writing about now?"

"Nothing," she said, squinting harder at her computer as if she would see the rest of her sentence in the distance and be able to wrangle it back into her head.

"Well, you should probably write *something*."

"Yeah, love to," she responded, annoyed. He reached up to stroke her hand.

"Can you just not?" she snapped. "If you want to take me wherever the hell you're taking me I have to actually work, Henry. This is my job."

He put his hands up, as if to say, "I didn't do it."

"Okay, Tess, I'll leave you alone. Just tell me what you feel."

"What I feel? Right now? Really fucking annoyed at you for not respecting that I asked you for space today. I know you just live your life and do whatever you want all the time, but sometimes that's just plain selfish. What you do affects other people."

"You feel disrespected."

"YES. I feel disrespected. And annoyed. *At you*," she fired off. Realizing he was not firing back, she slightly backed down. "And at me, for pushing this deadline and not being more responsible."

"Mmm. I see. I'm sorry I disrespected your boundary."

Tess looked at him, quizzically. Was this a fight? It could not possibly be this civil, this direct. She felt slightly ashamed of how hard she'd come at him when he did not return her fire.

"Sorry. I don't think you're selfish. I don't know why I said that. I just felt like you should have known how I feel."

"I don't always know how you feel, but if you just tell me, most of the rest sorts itself out. We tell each other how we feel, own our own parts of hurt and apologize. It doesn't have to all be so hard, you know. I'll leave you to your writing," he said, kissing her cheek again before disappearing into the garden.

Her interrupted thought about respect reappeared in her head as if he'd unlocked the door it was hiding behind. She carried on, completing the current chapter she'd promised Edgar and another half of the next.

Finally seated on the train to the beach, Tess silently stared out the window, letting her eyes rock back and forth, following the scenery as it sped by.

The trip had been less than ideal so far. As it turned out, Henry was a bit of a hurried traveler, something that inherently annoyed Tess. She found herself responding in terse monosyllabic responses, and sometimes not at all. She couldn't find the feeling and wasn't sure how to approach "you're annoying me!" in Henry's emotionally mature conversation rubric.

He seemed to be having fun so far, finding the fact that they almost missed their train to be significantly more comical than Tess did. Not even thirty minutes into their trip it felt that their bubble was bursting at the seams.

"You don't really know someone until you travel with them," Tess's mom had said one day, just after Jake and Tess got engaged. They had, of course, never really traveled together. Good Christian couples can't sleep together, so there were no romantic trips. No hotel lounging. No opportunity for them to learn how they work together in planning logistics and handling potentially stressful situations without completely snapping at each other. Tess's mom had always been a fan of the relationship, but there also seemed to be a hint of caution that they were jumping into something as serious as marriage without truly knowing each other.

Henry sat close, but not touching her. He seemed to sense her frustration but didn't try to talk or distract her from her feelings. This would be a moment when Tess may have appreciated the distraction, as frustration with Henry was a fairly new and unpleasant state. As their train pulled into Bordeaux, the words finally came.

"I hate to be rushed. It makes me so frazzled and irritable. I don't want to be short with you. It just feels like my whole body tenses up so hard I might explode. I know it's not cute and being uptight about timing and planning isn't super attractive. I wish I was more spontaneous and carefree, but I'm just not."

"I hear you, *chérie*. I am learning you. I can prevent us from being rushed. I'm sorry."

The wheels of the train screeched so loudly she shuddered, and then quieted. She breathed out. Clear, honest, respectful communication was something so foreign to her it felt like cheating for this to be the entire conversation. Like she shouldn't be allowed to use his conflict rubric against him.

"Yeah. Thanks. I mean, I appreciate it," she tried. "Sorry, you are throwing me off a bit."

"How do you mean?"

"This kind of just feels too easy? Like I just tell you how I feel, you validate me and apologize and that's it?"

"For this? Yes, that's it. Should there be more?"

She shook her head and kissed him. The seams of their bubble eased.

While waiting for the next train, Henry had been recognized—something Tess should have been but was completely unprepared for. The Henry who gets ogled by teenage girls was the same Henry she slept next to every night. Tess couldn't sort out if she admired this or felt a little slighted that the world got the same Henry Tate she did.

"Oh *mon dieu*! Oh *mon dieu*!!" two teenage girls shrieked, slapping each other in the arm and pointing at them. Tess had done a full 360 searching for what they were pointing at before she realized it was Henry. Even in his sunglasses and backward hat—a particularly uncharacteristic look for him—he had been spotted. Unaware of her role in this situation she shrunk back as he approached the screaming girls.

"*C'est un plaisir de vous rencontrer les filles. Une photo? Ah, bien sûr!*" He chatted with them for a few minutes with such ease, asking their names, what they're learning in school, if they had any good ideas for songs. Charm always felt like a difficult characteristic to mix with genuineness, but the blend of the two made the man completely magnetic. When the girls' train arrived, he kissed them each on the cheek and coolly headed back to Tess's side.

"So, you're famous, huh?" she asked, still facing away from him but unable to restrain her smile.

"A bit. Sometimes. Depends where I am. Do you mind?"

She turned to face him. "Not as long as you're you."

The second train ride was much more enjoyable than the first. Henry pretend-narrated the scenery out the window in his best BBC announcer voice. Tess remained tucked up under his arm with her hand casually resting on his leg. It all felt so normal aside from the sunglasses Henry insisted on wearing to damper the possibility of another fan interaction. They hadn't fully discussed how Tess was to handle these encounters, and they both silently hoped they wouldn't have to create a game plan. If they acted normal, maybe they would be seen as normal.

Lège-Cap-Ferret was, indeed, gorgeous. The sleepy beach town matched the essence of Henry, which made Tess instantly taken with the place. It was beautiful, peaceful, interesting. Their one-bedroom villa sat right on the edge of the sand leading up to the blue-green water. It was small but had to have cost more than Tess would ever pay for a place to sleep for a weekend. Instead, Henry had booked the place, insisting that it was his gift to her for completing her tenth chapter.

Inside they silently unpacked, side by side. Traveling drained her, always, and the ups and downs of the day had sucked the lighthearted playfulness they usually had right out of them. For the first time since their lives collided, they were "off."

Tess had yet to broach the topic of the Maria and Jo visit. She meant to! She meant to immediately, of course, but didn't yet have the vision for how she was going to explain Henry to them or how to explain to him that they didn't *exactly* know who he was. When she thought she found the words, she instead felt the urge to clean a bunch of dishes. Another time she was about to relay the information, Henry got a sudden moment of inspiration and began furiously writing on his notepad. So, now, a week had gone by with only a week until they were here, and Henry didn't know a thing about it.

"We've got dinner in an hour," he finally said, snapping her back to the present. "On a sunset sail."

"Mmm," she responded, barely registering the words.

"Did I tell you I have to go to Paris for a band meeting with our manager? It's like a week and a half away, and I've barely thought about it. Just realizing I should probably be more prepared than I am."

She nodded, unable to get on his conversation level.

"Tess where are you?" he asked, always aware when he wasn't getting the full her. Tinged with a tone of annoyance.

"Sorry—it's just been a long day and my brain is elsewhere."

"I see that—where is it?"

Tess sighed, effectively giving up. "My friends are coming to visit next weekend. I didn't tell you…because they don't really know about you. I'm excited they're coming, and I really want them to meet you, but I just don't know how to go about all of it."

"I see," he responded, sitting down on the bed as if the air had been knocked out of him. The admission clearly stirred up his feelings.

"It just feels like it's going to force us into the real world, and I don't want to be in the real world. I don't want to have to actually talk about what we're doing and what this is and when it's going to end. I am living in blissful, unlabeled heaven with you, and I'm scared of that changing," she blurted out, desperate to remove the hurt she'd already caused. It was the truth, and a fairly thorough explanation of her feelings. Just not nearly as tactful as the speech she had been rehearsing if she'd ever found the right moment on her own to broach this with him.

Tess studied Henry's face as he digested her words, letting them sink in before responding. The creases by his eyes indicated a slight pain at this whole discussion, although she didn't know if she had caused it or if he was preparing for the pain *he* would cause. She joined him on the bed and took his face in her hands.

"Look. We don't have to decide anything right now, or even really talk about this. I'm sorry I didn't tell you sooner."

"We can talk about it later if you'd like. I don't have a lot of answers for you yet. But I do need you to know that I want to be with you like I haven't ever wanted to be with anyone before." He was so stern, so serious that Tess almost had to look away. "I don't want to *have* you—I've had plenty of women and then I move on. I know I want to just *be* with you. I don't know what that looks like. But if this is what you want too, we can sort out the details later."

Her breath caught as she finally remembered to exhale and realized her eyes had widened to half her face. Part of the avoidance of having this conversation was that she didn't want to know what his answer would be. If this wasn't as real to him as it was to her she would be crushed, destroyed by the weight she had inadvertently put on their non-relationship. But if he did feel the same, if he wanted to be with her? That proved an even more difficult situation.

This was confirmation that they both wanted what they could not have. As true as this was, she couldn't bear to say it out loud, and especially not now. Instead she softened her eyes, pulled his beautiful face toward hers and kissed him.

Tess had never been on a trip planned for her. She was used to being in charge and was comfortable being the one to make decisions. As frustrated as she always felt toward Jake for being incapable of making plans for them and following through, she found herself out of her element following someone else's plans for her weekend.

Late again, they arrived at their scheduled sunset sail just before the boat pushed off, and scrambled to get on while muttering *"désolé, désolé, désolé"* on a loop. Chronic lateness was on Tess's list of red flags, and she fought to not hold this against him for the sake of this romantic setup. With Henry's arm around her as the evening chilled, champagne in her hand and a gorgeous sunset, she could find very little to be mad about.

Once anchored in the open water, they were seated at a tiny table at the bow of the boat as a white-gloved man served their dinner and more champagne. This was so over the top of any experience Tess had had before that she could not stop giggling. Henry was clearly quite pleased with himself.

"To France," he said as they clinked their glasses, each plastered with competing wide grins.

"Is this the sort of thing you do often?" she finally asked, reckoning with the lack of understanding she had of what his real life actually looked like outside Abzac.

He smiled coyly. "No, not often. Are you asking if you're the first woman I've taken on a sunset dinner sail?"

"No—well, not exactly. I think I'd rather not know the answer to that. I'm just realizing how little I know about what your real life looks like outside of here. This is so much more extravagant than anything I've ever done, and now I'm wondering if we've got an ocean between the luxury of your life and the practicality of mine."

He pondered this. Tess admired his thoughtful responses, but sometimes wondered what would shoot out of his mouth upon instinct if he did not always think so thoroughly before speaking.

"I don't really know what my actual life looks like anymore. When I started becoming successful and was making really shitty decisions, I was like a new, worse person. Consumed with drugs, women, parties, buying shit. I know *about* a lot of things that happened, but I don't have many sensory memories before rehab. Like I was so numb I wasn't present for any of the wild experiences

I was having. I'm a little nervous to go back, really. I don't exactly know what my life looks like back in the real world."

"Well. What are the things you know you want to be part of your real life?"

Dimples. "You want me to make a Tess list and pin it to my fridge?"

She chuckled. "Kind of, I guess. It just sounds like you have this beautiful opportunity to rebuild your life, and I'm curious what you want it to look like."

He obviously enjoyed this question.

"I want to see my family more often. Spend some time with Aunt Rita. I want to meditate daily and read a lot and just sit and listen to music while doing absolutely nothing else. I certainly want to write songs. Performing is fun, but writing is my real passion. Maybe that's where I'll land after this album, as a writer in the background rather than a center-stage artist. We'll see.

"I actually think I want to leave London, but I'm not sure where I want to go. Part of this is deciding how far I want to lean into being in the public eye. I don't love fame, but I don't hate it, and I'm not sure how well it fits into the other things I want in my life. I want to be a dad. I want to host dinner parties. I want to keep meeting with my therapist." He closed his eyes and faced the moon, appearing like he, himself was glowing. "I'd like to see you in my real life," he added, keeping his eyes closed.

The jolt of joy that shot through Tess's body nearly threw her out of her seat. The knowledge that he thought of her outside of their French faux life was exhilarating, but beyond what she was prepared to discuss in this conversation, and she found herself scrambling to identify what she was feeling and how she should respond.

"I'm sure that could be arranged," was the most she could muster. This conversation felt like a wolf that had been chasing them for weeks and was now at the point of nipping at their ankles. It was only a matter of time before it was completely unavoidable. But not tonight.

Soft music wafted up to the bow of the boat from the live violinist, playing just for them.

"Dance with me?" she asked, unable to elaborate on her noncommittal response for the time being.

"Always," he promised.

Swaying cheek to cheek, Tess was overcome by the perfection of the moment.

"There's nothing I want that I don't have right now," she whispered to him. He drew back, holding her gaze, marveling at her with awe.

Somehow, vacation Henry was even more laid back than French-countryside Henry. He sauntered around their villa in the nude, sipped his coffee all day and took lots of naps. They didn't end up doing very much except reading, eating, drinking and having lots of sex. The change of scenery was nice, though.

Eventually craving fresh air, they strolled hand in hand on the beach, down the cobblestone streets, in and out of shops—romantic scene after romantic scene with a perfect man she was falling completely in love with. Tess liked the feel of them in the real world and couldn't help but notice the attention they received. She had never been with a man so beautiful and feared that the eyes of others that seemed to constantly follow them were borne out of disbelief rather than envy.

The conversation about their status in the real world sat right below the surface, remaining just out of sight, but palpably there.

By the end of the weekend their bubble hadn't burst, it had solidified. Pressure and timelines and input from the outside world pushed in, but then the rebuild was only stronger. Tess didn't want to live in a fragile bubble. She wanted a cozy cocoon they built around themselves, strong because of the storms they had weathered. She knew now in the core of her body and mind that she could not imagine this was a temporary thing.

The train ride home was quiet, dreamy, comfortable. Henry held her close, avoiding eye contact with strangers who could recognize him. They floated home together in their cocoon, unbothered by the long late-night walk home from the train station.

Henry abruptly stopped at her cottage, letting go of her hand.

"Sleep here tonight. I'm going to sleep at my cottage."

The rate at which her stomach dropped instinctively sent her hand to her belly as if to hold her body in place. This was the first time either of them had ever suggested taking space. Her mind raced with things she could have done wrong that would have put him off.

"Darling, breathe. I am looking forward to meeting your friends, however you decide you want that to look. Right now I need a little time on my own. I need to sort out my feelings and priorities and such." *Breathe, two, three, four.* "I can't deny it, Tess. I love you. I have fallen totally and completely in love with you. Please don't say anything yet. I know you're not ready to have this conversation. So, I am taking a little space. Come by for dinner tomorrow night. I love you."

She remained frozen, stunned. His casual delivery did not correlate to the tsunami she felt flowing through her at these words. Pure joy and bliss washed over her in tandem with deep fear of hurt. The two were intertwined, as if there were no option for one on its own at this point. She felt simultaneously on cloud nine and in the bottom of a pit.

He kissed her cheek, squeezed her hand with a knowing smile, and turned to walk down the road.

Tess felt oddly out of place in a house she was supposed to be living in. Henry's home had become her home, and, to her dismay, had also become the home of her typewriter and laptop. She needed some way to get her words out. Digging through her luggage she came up with a broken pencil and the last few pages from her almost full legal pad. There was enough space to unpack, and she began furiously writing.

A tiny seed, planted
Watered, nurtured, rooted
Creeping up the side of the house, delicately covering the cracks
Winding up, over around
Nestling in the nooks of the plaster
Growing up, over, faster
The house is gone
The ivy lives
Once a pretty plant, now a disaster

She knew two things without a doubt: she was absolutely, unequivocally in love with Henry.

And she absolutely, unequivocally could not tell him.

The next night Tess pulled out her yellow dress. The weather was slightly too cold for it, but it complemented her beach weekend tan perfectly. It also said for her what she couldn't say for herself: *I love you too.*

She grabbed a few dahlias from the garden and long grasses to form a makeshift bouquet and headed back down the lane. The pulling in her chest felt magnetic, like her heart was leading her down the road to him. She'd never recognized the feeling of yearning before, but it felt like every part of her was desperate to be back closer to him.

As she approached, Tess could see him sitting outside, sipping rosé in a patterned button-down shirt tucked into rolled slacks. The formality of this dinner had not been discussed, but they somehow both knew they needed to show up for each other. He stood immediately when he saw her, quickly making his way in her direction.

"*Chérie*," he said, showing up her wide smile with his own wider one. He picked her up and spun her around, her yellow linen dress swirling around them. They kissed deeply but briefly.

"I missed you," she offered first.

"I missed you. I'm all better now."

"You look perfect," she said, kissing his face. They walked with arms wrapped around each other tightly, back into his house and back into their life together.

October

Seventeen

"Lugging this bag is literally harder than climbing Mt. Kilimanjaro," Maria groaned as they finally approached the dirt road of the estate. She would know, having hiked in Tanzania the summer after law school. Maria's absolute innate badassness, however, still came with ample complaining. Even Jo the CrossFit queen was sweating a bit under her pack, but she straightened up and powered through whenever Tess caught her eye.

"This is the estate. My cottage is just a little further down this road." More groans.

Tess had biked to the train station in Coutras to pick up her shrieking entourage. Their reunion reeked of American obnoxiousness, and Tess was glad Henry wasn't there to witness the scene. Being around her old home friends, she reverted to acting the same as she did when they were fifteen.

The walk had given Tess time to casually drop the "I live with Henry" overview she had taken hours to painstakingly refine to be honest enough without sending her friends into a tizzy.

"Tess," was all Maria could manage. She never lied, and Tess never had to guess what she thought about something. There was a comfort in that. To Maria, this fling seemed to be nothing but a mistake that would end in totally avoidable pain. She wouldn't say it, not yet, but she also wouldn't lie.

"Oh my god, this is exciting! I can't wait to meet him," Jo followed, forever the hype man of the group. Tess felt both things as well—deeply excited about the quasi-life they had built here and cautiously fearful as she marched to the inevitable end.

Henry, on the other hand, was overjoyed to meet her friends. He had heard glimpses of meetings with Edgar, thus far the only peek into what Tess's actual life looked like. She had mostly communicated with her family by postcard, with a few texts to Luke. Maria and Jo were real-life representations of so much of who Tess was. And to be frank, they were a lot.

A rotating soundtrack of oohs and ahhs and whines and groans accompanied the entire walk to her cottage. They would be staying at Tess's cottage; an odd place to host her friends when she had actually spent such little time there herself. Henry's cottage felt like home, but nothing would dampen this reunion more than Tess's love interest hanging around in his gorgeous, clothes-resistant body.

Out of habit, Tess popped on a pot of tea as they came inside, which Maria and Jo had to immediately make fun of.

"Teatime, huh? What even is your life out here?"

Tess ignored the jab.

"I have snacky charcuterie stuff here, but for dinner, we're going to Henry's," she stated, matter-of-factly as she'd planned. She kept her eyes on the tea she was pouring but could see the glances her friends exchanged out of her periphery.

"Dude, what is going on. You are being weird and cryptic, and we've barely heard two words about this guy before today. You're living with him? He's making us dinner tonight? Who *is* he to you?" Maria couldn't help herself but ask.

This is what Tess wanted to avoid: questions she did not have answers for quite yet. She breathed, bit off a large piece of baguette and poured the tea.

"Let's sit outside," she offered, even though the chill was slightly too cold for comfort. They tossed their bags down, grabbed their cups and followed her to the terrace.

Tess always thought more clearly outside. Something about the air made her words flow smoother, truer, less reserved.

"So, Henry. I met him early on, and we spent a whole weekend together. I don't think I've ever…I can't believe I'm saying this shit. I've never had a connection like I do with him. Intellectually, emotionally, physically. All of it. We tried to get it out of our systems. It didn't work, and we sort of fell back into spending all our time together. I don't know what he is to me. I just know that while I'm here I want to be with him." She paused, sipped, continued. "He's a singer and lives in London. We know there's no future for us outside of here. And it's not like I'm looking for a relationship right now. But, for here, he's perfect."

Each woman silently sipped her tea in an effort to tactfully collect their thoughts before responding.

"And you're not just sleeping with him? It's like a real thing with feelings and he's going to meet your best friends?" Maria asked.

"I mean, yeah, there are feelings. He told me he loved me the other day. But we haven't really talked about what this actually is and where it goes from here. It's so drastically less controlled than any romantic relationship I've ever encountered. Which I think I'm okay with, for now."

"So then when you leave in a few weeks you just get wrecked? We know you, Tess. This is going to crush you."

Tess let that sit a minute as Jo took a giant gulp of tea. Maria was probably right—Maria was always right. But even if she was, Tess felt such a sense of pride in her lack of desire to control this situation. It was freeing—exactly what she came here to be. Letting go of designing outcomes and letting herself fall. Even if she did get hurt.

"It might. I don't know. We haven't talked it all out. I have no expectations. I am honestly just trusting my gut and feeling however I feel without overanalyzing everything. I get the protective response, but I'm actually proud of myself for letting go of that control."

Jo nodded in agreement, easing Tess's defenses.

"Look. This man has been my whole life here. I am enjoying my time with him, and I just thought you guys might enjoy time with him too. He's unlike anyone I've ever met. It's not a big pressure meeting where I'm looking for your thoughts or approval. He's just cool and fun and a significantly better cook than me. And he's a singer, so we might get a little show."

"Oh wow! That's very cool. Like that's his real job?" Jo asked.

"Yeah. He's a bit famous over here. I'd never heard of him, but he's gotten recognized a few times and it's so wild to me."

"Wait—what's his last name?" Maria asked. Tess had specifically been trying to avoid any of their influence and judgment, and the thought that Maria may have already heard some (likely negative) things about Henry caused her stomach to turn so fast she was thrust forward. Swatting at a non-existent bug by her leg she played off the scene, buying herself a few extra seconds.

"Tate," Tess responded, tersely. She struggled to recall the name as she'd used it so seldomly. She had even avoided Googling him for fear of ruining the Henry she knew.

"Henry Tate. You're dating Henry Tate," Maria repeated, slowly. Her eyes gave her thoughts away. She knew of him. Maria was a pop culture queen and knew about everyone. Her opinions formed and dried like concrete, nearly impossible to shift.

"I mean no, not really. But yeah, it's Henry Tate. You've heard of him?"

Tess could sense Jo panicking, having run out of tea to hide behind. This was about to be the kind of confrontational conversation Jo would typically excuse herself from, often faking a call from her wife. Here, with no distractions and obvious tensions on the line, she would have no choice but to sit and clench her jaw until Tess and Maria worked it out. Jo's panic caused Tess to tense even further, bracing for the tongue-thrashing that was inevitably coming from Maria.

"Yep," Maria answered after a few seconds. "I have questions," she added, pulling her phone out of her pocket. "What's the Wi-Fi?"

"It barely works and I'm not telling you. Maria. I don't need to Google the man. I've spent most of the last six weeks with him. I'd bet that anything you could show me I've already heard. And if not, I honestly don't even care. I need you to chill. I'm not marrying this person, I'm sleeping with him on my solo vacation in France and having an amazing fucking time for maybe the first time in my entire life. I'm not looking for input on this decision."

Tess had expected word vomit in this conversation, but more likely from Maria than herself. Jo's eyes widened and she raised her empty teacup to her lips again.

Maria slowly nodded. Tess exhaled.

In twenty years of friendship, she had never asserted herself this strongly to Maria and had no blueprint for what would happen next. *In two-three-four, hold two-three-four, out two-three-four, hold two-three-four.*

"Okay. Well, we're here. Might as well go meet the fucker," she said, standing. This time Jo and Tess exchanged glances, both seemingly relieved that this conversation stayed civil and was now over.

The women settled into Tess's room for their extended weekend stay. Tess plopped down on the sofa, her bed for the weekend, since sharing a bed with her friends seemed to prevent her body from producing an ounce of melatonin. Sleeping at Henry's wasn't an option she considered, but she did find herself sliding her hand up and down the couch cushion as if it were his chest. Like her body just expected to be near his.

Maria and Jo had flown on a plane for hours, sat on a train and dragged their packs down the final stretch to the house. Showers were required at this point, understandably, but Tess couldn't help but notice Maria layering on eyeliner and perfume, which would not be her normal routine for an at-home dinner. The Henry effect was already setting in and they hadn't even met him.

As the time until dinner disappeared, Tess found her nerves heightening, crawling into the crevices of her whole body. She had pitched an unruffled demeanor about this dinner, but as reality set in she couldn't deny the weight of importance of this for her.

As much as she wanted to remove pressure from the weekend, she couldn't avoid the lightning bolt pang of anxiety that shot through her stomach as she pictured walking down the lane, Henry's face when he opened the door, Maria and Jo's body language upon meeting him.

"This will be good," she told herself.

"Huh?" asked Jo, poking her head out of Tess's room.

"Ah, nothing." She'd need to dial back the habit of talking to herself. "You guys about ready?"

By the time the crew was packed up and ready to walk the hundred yards down the road, they were already fifteen minutes late. This, Tess would admit, was a staple of her real life back home when it came to events with her friends. She just couldn't find the assertiveness to get their asses together on time.

"Do we look okay?" Jo asked, earnestly. Tess was touched by how seriously they were taking this dinner, even if she herself didn't know how to take it.

"You guys look amazing. Let's do it," Tess assured them.

Henry greeted them at the door in a lovely pink button-down shirt with a dish towel over his shoulder. Music streamed from the record player, and four glasses of wine were already poured and at the table. Tess couldn't help the joy she felt by how seriously he seemed to be taking this too.

"Welcome, *les filles américaines*! I'm Henry." He leaned in to air kiss the two women, before pulling Tess in for a real kiss. She was so flushed she couldn't turn back to meet their eyes, as this was more PDA than they'd ever seen from her even after ten years with Jake.

"Come in, come in!" he continued, clearly playing The Most Gracious Host Who Ever Lived.

"Thank you so much for having us," Jo responded, putting out her hand like she'd just arrived at an important business meeting. "I'm Jo. It's great to meet you." Henry shook her hand with matching earnestness, which only Tess recognized as done in jest.

"Maria," Maria casually threw over her shoulder without actually turning to address him as she sauntered into his home.

Sorry, Jo mouthed to Henry, who seemed to be unable to wipe the smile off his face.

"Well, lovely to have you both. I've made a curry, hope that suits you. It's pretty much a staple for us here. Oh, and wine, of course," he offered, just as Maria was taking her first sip.

"This is so nice," Jo kept repeating. The juxtaposition of Maria's hard-to-please demeanor with Jo's far-too-easy-to-please was comical. Henry and Tess agreed with their eyes, without needing to verbalize what they were both experiencing.

"Please, sit," Henry offered, gesturing to the chairs. "Dinner is just about ready. I don't want to take up your night—I know you have such limited time together. I just wanted to meet you and feed you. Not that our sweet Tess couldn't have handled that on her own..." He trailed off cheekily. Even Maria smiled at that one, as "Tess can't cook" jokes came by the dozen in their friendship.

"So what are you doing here, Henry?" Maria asked, lifting her voice slightly at the end to suggest a question rather than an accusation.

"Same as Tess. Working. Writing mostly, singing loudly. I play music."

"I know," Maria responded. Henry's face visibly shifted as he seemingly flipped through the possibilities of what she may already know about him. He busied his hands.

"Would you play something for us?" Jo chimed in. There was no better counterbalance for Maria's hard exterior than Jo's mushy softness.

Henry smiled. "I've got five more minutes on the rice—I'll play you one. I wrote it about Tess, actually. I've been pretty inspired since she's been around."

Tess thought she caught Maria rolling her eyes but chose to ignore it.

Henry picked up his guitar and began the familiar "*dada da da*" melody she had grown to love. It really had stuck, and for all its simplicity it made her feel, deeply. He played through "Sunbeam." Maria's body language seemed to soften a bit. At the end, enthusiastic applause from all three women filled the cottage.

"That was actually really good. So, what do you find so 'inspiring' about our Tess?" Maria asked.

"I promise I have perfect, completely unplanned answers to your prying questions but let me just put the curry out first. All my answers will be significantly more satisfying if your stomach is full," he called back over his shoulder. Maria lifted her eyebrows at Tess who could only laugh, shrugging her shoulders. His charm worked on everyone, even a tough nut to crack like Maria.

Once they were all set at the table and had tucked into their dinner, Henry brought the question back.

"So. What inspires me about Tess. Well, I don't know what you know from her side, but I'm happy to give you mine. I saw Tess across a lake one day. From the moment she walked over and sat beside me, I wanted to be near her. I don't know how to explain it other than a hokey cosmic connection. But I do know myself, and what I feel. I felt simultaneously at peace and in awe, struck by this person." He held her gaze, totally unselfconscious in pouring out his heart. "I think I'm most inspired by the way she looks at life. That she questions things like she's trying to squeeze every drop out of her existence. That she knows who she is and what she believes. I work in an industry where staying true to yourself is difficult, and being around a person like Tess just makes it easier. I could not find a single reason to stay away from her as long as we're here—"

"As long as you're here," Maria interrupted, highlighting the reality. Of all the glorious, beautiful things he had said about her, Maria caught the one she was looking for.

"Yes," he confirmed coolly, confidently. "We know this thing has an expiration date. We won't live together in our regular lives the way we live together here. There will be change, and we haven't figured out exactly what that will look like yet."

"But I mean, come on, Maria, even you have to admit that was gorgeous," Jo chimed in with her best puppy dog eyes.

"Of course. Gorgeous. Trust me, we love Tess. We're just looking out for her."

"And I appreciate that," Tess finally interjected. "But now I'm uncomfortable with how much the conversation has been about me. Maria, Jo, fill us in. What's going on in the real world?"

Henry's hand squeezed her knee under the table. The test was over, and at least for now, he'd passed.

The rest of the night was lighter, fun. More reflective of the time Henry and Tess usually spent together. Henry took Jo's hand and pulled her up to dance with him, which led her to question her own sexuality and sent the four of them into a laughing fit. By the time they stood to leave they were all tipsy, full and happy. Even Maria had settled into herself and decided to enjoy the evening.

"It was so nice to meet you. I hope we see you again," Jo gushed at the door.

"I'll make sure of it," Henry responded, winking.

Maria kissed his cheeks and pulled him in for a hug no one was expecting.

"We're rooting for you," she half-drunk loud-whispered in his ear as if Tess couldn't hear.

"Me too," he said back.

The rest of the weekend was laid back. The loud, American trio trekked into town to visit Didier's store, mostly to understand the stories Tess had told of the place and to believe it for themselves. They lounged on the terrace and drank wine from morning till night, never running out of topics to cover.

Laughing with her friends about absolutely nothing felt like it restored a piece of Tess she'd been missing since being here. Even the perfect man could not replace the need for genuine female friendships.

On their last night, the women all sat on Tess's bed, packing everything up.

"You guys, I can't even begin to thank you for coming here. This was amazing. I wish we had more time," Tess started.

"We had an idea," Jo admitted. The quick shift of Maria's face indicated that this had been discussed, there was a plan, and Jo was not approaching the topic the way she had foreseen it.

"Mhmmm..." Tess responded, hesitantly.

"We think you need to be with us for a while after you come home," Jo continued. "You can't go to your parents' house, and I really don't think you should be alone back in your apartment. You've spent months alone. Or—I guess not really, but not with people who really know you. So, we worked out some plans for you. Which we know is not your favorite thing, but it's for your own good."

Maria shot Jo a look, clearly frustrated at the delivery of said plan. Tess's face certainly had given her away, as her eyebrows could not hide the discomfort she felt at having her life planned for her.

"Yeah," Maria said curtly, turning to Tess. "Well, you have a bunch of obligations in New York when you get back anyway. Steve and I have the extra bedroom, and he's traveling a lot for work right now. Just figured it would be cool if you came to stay with us for a month or so until you've got your next steps figured out in Maryland."

"And then you can come to Portland!" Jo offered, excitedly. "We have the space, and Liz could use an extra person to cook for. We're not going back to Maryland for Christmas this year anyway, so you could stay through the holidays. We were thinking of heading up to Bar Harbor actually. What do you think?"

Tess had not given thorough thought to life after France. She had her landlord's emails to re-up the lease on her dingy apartment, fractured pieces of a relationship with a family who thought she was poison, and an ex-husband. Gallivanting around New England for the winter with her favorite people didn't sound like a half-bad plan.

"Guys, that is really so kind. Let me think about it, okay?"

"You think about it," Maria answered. "I'll book us a table at Shukette for the week you come back," she added, slyly.

Tess could not suppress her smile at the way her friends loved her. She had yet to fully acknowledge how soon she'd be leaving here, and as much as she was not ready to let go of Henry, the comfort of being caught by her best people softened the blow, at least for now.

After Maria and Jo were safely deposited at the train station, Tess's body urged her to run to Henry's house. He would be leaving in the morning for his meeting with his meeting in Paris. The time she had spent with her friends was precious, but the end of her time with Henry loomed and she would not waste it. Her feet could not carry her fast enough, and she arrived covered in sweat after running what was likely her fastest mile ever.

❦

The next morning, tangled up in his sheets, they both lay there avoiding the inevitable.

"Fuck. I have to go. I don't want to go," he said, over and over.

"I know. Time is a thief. I can't believe we're already here. Hurry and go so you can hurry back."

This seemed to be motivation enough. With impressive speed, Henry threw some fairly nice clothes in his bag and grabbed a piece of toast. She walked him to the door, too sleepy and naked to get him all the way to the station and on his way for three days of album release meetings in Paris. It was all for the music, of course, but Tess found it hard to throw her full enthusiasm behind the trip if it meant time apart. As much as she wanted him to go off and be himself, she wanted him for her as well.

After what she thought was their final goodbye, Henry turned back to face her.

"I love you, Tess. I know it doesn't change anything in the grand scheme of all of this. I've loved people before, and I know love doesn't necessarily mean a life together. I just need you to know," he stated, matter-of-factly. He hadn't brought this up since the night they returned from Cap-Ferret, and although it felt good to hear, it also complicated things so deeply that she wished he'd stop saying it.

She knew it was true. Even before he ever said it. She knew it from the day she found him singing outside her door.

She also knew that she felt the same. Almost the same. She definitely loved him, that had been apparent for weeks. What she didn't know was whether love like this could possibly *not* mean a life together.

Even without a vision of what a real relationship could look like, she had a harder time imagining a life without him. Afraid of what could come out of her mouth, she pressed it up to his, telling him she loved him back with her hands instead of her words.

Eighteen

The days without Henry dragged on, but Tess found the space fruitful for her actual job. She pored into her writing, as if working hard would make him come back faster. The minutes still ticked by seemingly half-time. Her productivity doubled.

After three days Henry was back and eager to make up for lost time.

The pressure was building as their expiration date barreled toward them. As always after time apart they clicked back together like Lego pieces. This particular reunion held more passion than ever, and they finished in a pile of limbs on his bed.

As desperate as Tess was to know what was going through his mind as they lay together in silence, she couldn't bring herself to ask. If she asked, she would know, and she wasn't sure she wanted to know. Even without words, she could feel that he was elsewhere. That something was different. That the shine of their magic had dimmed, or at least been eclipsed by his brief time back in his own real life.

After another five full minutes marked by soft exhales, Henry finally broke the silence.

"I can't believe you leave next week. I wish we could stay here forever," he mused as he traced her ribs with his finger.

"Maybe it's time to talk about this," she offered, half-heartedly. His arched eyebrow didn't stop her but didn't exactly portray agreement.

"I don't really know what our options are," she continued, honestly. Although this conversation had been coming for months, she never felt even a second of relief from the tension of the rock and hard place they were in. "We both have commitments. I'm more flexible. I would never ask you to give up everything you've worked so hard for." Tess paused, allowing him the opportunity to fill in the next sentence. He remained silent; eyes glued to the ceiling.

"I don't know how, Henry. But I don't want to be without you," she finally finished, falling just short of the admission that she did, in fact, love him. That she wanted to be with him. Whatever that looked like. She waited, but he said nothing.

Tess threw her leg over his to flip herself onto his chest and pushed up to meet his eyes. If he wasn't going to meet hers, she would come to him.

Months of staring deep into each other's eyes made it all too comfortable to do this and both remain silent. She hadn't anticipated silence from him, and already felt way out on a limb with what she had admitted, but too scared to jump all the way off for fear he wouldn't catch her. At this point it didn't feel like he was even on the same planet as her, much less in the same room pinned to the bed by her naked body.

He let out an audible, frustrated breath. "I don't know what you want me to say, Tess. I've told you I love you. We both know there aren't actually viable options to do this outside of this place. Not unless one of us gives up the life we built for ourselves. And I don't think either of us wants to do that after how hard we fought to *be* ourselves. However we feel about each other is magic. But that doesn't mean there is room for magic in the real world."

The conversation was getting farther from what she imagined by the second. A burning sensation welled up in her chest, much like the knot of rage she used to suppress before unleashing on her punching bag. She quickly assessed the mad, found its roots in fear and abandonment and self-doubt, and went in.

"Say it, Henry. Say you don't want me to come on tour with you." The burning sensation intensified, fueling some masochistic need she had to hear the dagger of his honest words.

"I don't want you to come on tour with me. And *you* don't want to come on tour with me. This has a hard expiration date."

It hit differently than she expected it to, eliciting more anger than sadness. Anger at him for letting it get this far and telling her he loved her. Hotter anger at herself, for *knowing* from the start that this was the only way this would end, and still allowing herself to believe that there was a way.

He shook his head and gently rolled her off of him to sit up.

"We both know I can't bring you into that world, Tess. It is bad and you are good. You're a sunbeam, and that's beautiful, but your sunshiny heart couldn't handle the world I live in. Shit, the worst thing you've ever done is throw a CD out a window," he muttered, pulling on his pants and standing as if this was a reasonable time to walk away.

She briefly grappled with whether he was unaware or didn't care about how swiftly and deeply that cut her. The entanglement of guilt and shame and confrontation of her own "goodness" twisted into a blade so sharp it sliced right through her.

"I fucking lied," she blurted, eyes wide. He slowly turned around, seemingly cautious about the energy he would be greeted with. She was shaking; angry, sad, worried about what would happen when it was all out. He met her eyes and froze.

Suddenly it wasn't about their future, or the tour at all. He had boxed her in. Stuck her in a cute, tightly fitting prison of "good." Decided who she was and what she could do and decided wrong. With increasing heat building in her chest, she opened her mouth to speak three times before she could form her words.

She knew that in the same way she knew what would happen before she ever touched Henry. If she started she would not be able to stop. Searching for the same freedom that had come with Henry's touch, she let go.

"Jake and I didn't just get divorced because we were better apart. We should have, but we didn't. I couldn't. So I blew us up." She drew in a sharp breath. "We had been trying to get pregnant for years. I thought it just wasn't going to happen for us. We thought a baby and moving forward with our family was the thing that was missing for us, but I knew we were kidding ourselves.

"And then one day I took a test and it was positive. I freaked out. Made an appointment at the clinic that day. Got a swift abortion." It was hard to get her mouth to spit out those words. To call it what it was. For someone who grew up believing that abortion was the cardinal sin, even in her liberal, ex-vangelical reformation this was hard to admit.

"I didn't tell anyone. All I knew was I couldn't be connected to Jake forever. I had to get out. A week later I told him I had an abortion, and that I wanted a divorce. He left and it was done." She took a second. Was she breathing? Was he still listening? She couldn't bring herself to look at him to find out but kept her eyes glued to the floor and powered on.

"I was so cowardly and he didn't deserve it. I should have just told him I wanted a divorce without making him and me and our families and my body go through all of that. I knew it deep down, but I couldn't admit it until the test was positive. I actually said 'I want a divorce' out loud by myself in the bathroom as soon as I saw the two blue lines. I would have given anything to have had the courage to say it to him sooner."

Henry, in all of his warmth and sweetness and truth softly whispered, "And now, how do you feel?"

She let out an enormous breath she'd been holding in, releasing her shoulders and neck and sinking into the bed. "Shame. I feel like a fake. A total coward. I know the abortion was the right choice. I could not have had that baby and stayed in that life. I just feel so ashamed that it had to come to that for me to do the right thing and end the marriage. I fully blame myself, and it feels like I always will."

Compassion filled his eyes. She felt the hurt slightly lifting from her as he took it on too, giving her room to keep going.

"Jake wouldn't talk to me after I told him. I craved punishment in some masochistic attempt to get the wrath I deserved. So I drove to my parent's house and told them about the abortion, everything about the book and the divorce all at once. I don't know that I could have told them anything worse. My parents said such harsh things I don't know that I will ever see them again. They just kept saying they could not believe how much darkness was inside me. And I get what they mean." She drew another sharp breath in the chilly air. "I do have all this darkness in me. I try to give the world the best of myself, but I am no fucking sunbeam." There it was. The veil of fog around the darkest corner of Tess's life was lifted, and she sat in the rawest version of herself before Henry.

Her eyes scanned the seams in the wood floor until she mustered up the courage to meet his intense gaze. He kneeled by the bed and grasped her waist, supporting her body.

"Maybe not. But you are human. Which is much better."

She pressed her head against his, desperate for this to soak in and be true. Trying to transfer the way he saw her to the way she saw herself.

The relationship conversation remained unresolved, and neither one of them could bear to bring it up again. Carrying on as usual also seemed impossible. Instead, Henry and Tess spent their final week together watching the minutes tick by, empty, useless. Rather than soak up the last time they had together or cut the line early, they did nothing.

His band meetings had gone well, and Tess couldn't help but notice that Henry seemed different, distant. He focused solely on the music, even shutting himself in the bedroom for hours to work. She wondered if he noticed that he could walk by her without touching her, something that previously felt impossible.

He talked less and asked fewer questions. It felt like he stopped wandering into her and pulled back into himself. The path he had been foraging halted, so close to the center of her, but now abandoned.

She let it go, resolving that this would protect whatever was left of her ability to mitigate hurt. They each gently glided through their days, treating each other like vintage teacups they were terrified of breaking.

Tess's belongings disappeared from around Henry's cottage slowly but surely until they were all piled into her backpacking bag and suitcase by his front door. The pile of all her things seemed smaller than it should be, like the monumental experiences she'd had in the last several months should have added up to more. Instead, the little pile of all her things felt trivial, like she easily could clean up and remove all of her from his cottage and his life without leaving a trace.

Henry said nothing about it, and she wondered if he noticed or just wouldn't say anything, settling that neither was the better option. As swiftly and inevitably as the pile, their last night together arrived.

"Sorry I don't have anything nicer to make," he said over his shoulder as he scrambled omelets for them for their final dinner. She continued pouring their glasses of wine, which seemed to have doubled in size from the previous week.

"It's fine," she tossed back, having taken this approach to the entire situation. A nice dinner could not quantify their time together, and the night felt like more of a death march than a celebration.

They quietly set the table, seemingly avoiding eye contact. When he raised his glass to her she slightly jumped, so dissociated from the moment that she couldn't process the movement in her periphery. This clearly amused him, as he met her eyes for what felt like the first time that day.

"To Abzac. And this summer, and Antoinette, and to you, Tess. It's truly been an honor." They clinked their glasses solemnly, sans celebration. "I'm sorry I've been so distant the last week. I have no regrets about any minute I've spent with you here. I know we'll be alright; I am just dreading being without you and maybe trying to cushion that fall a bit. But this has all been…just…magic. So to magic, too, I guess."

He'd broken eye contact by the end in a seemingly self-protective move. Tess was also having trouble connecting with him in the here and now, finding herself aching to look away from him and send her mind elsewhere. This was going to be incredibly hard.

"To magic," she repeated as they clinked their glasses again. "Can we just be normal tonight?" she added, hoping to soak up every last bit of him before she left.

"Yes, I can be normal. I will be normal all the way up until you walk out this door, and then I'll be a mess. But, again, I have no regrets. This has all been very worth it to me."

"Me too," she murmured as she downed her wine.

Omelets and wine turned out to be the perfect dinner to end their three months in Abzac. They exchanged small anecdotal memories of their time, like markers along a map to where they were now and the depth of the connection they had built.

Henry mused on an insightful question she'd asked him. The time he woke up distressed and confused by her hair draped across his face. The day they'd shrieked and giggled trying to get a trapped bird out of the cottage.

Tess recounted the way he'd hummed her through an anxiety attack. How he'd sometimes wear her clothes. A zucchini dinner he'd made that she could finally admit she actually hated.

"Do you remember when you came over and sat next to me on the dock the day we met?" he asked with sparks of nostalgia in his glossy eyes. As if she could possibly forget.

"Mhmm. You didn't exactly invite me over."

"Ha. Not exactly, and I did notice you seemed to want to come over. Do you remember me sitting on my hands next to you? It was a wild thing. I had this feeling like I had to restrain myself, or I was going to touch you. I barely even knew your name yet, but I sort of felt like I couldn't control my body. Like it wanted to touch yours whether my brain was aware, or it was appropriate or not. Like my hands had a mind of their own."

She smiled. "I didn't notice you sitting on your hands. But I know what you mean. I'll tell you I don't understand how chemistry works between two people, but it felt like my body recognized something in yours right away too. Like it just clicked."

"Magic..." He trailed off, breaking eye contact as his glossy eyes turned teary. The end was visible.

They had been through this dance before, trying to soak up the last moments of each other before their inevitable separation. This time they couldn't be bothered to waste it with sleep, and stayed up the whole night talking, making love and holding on to each other tightly.

The morning sun streamed in, reaching Tess's eyelids just as she'd taken a few minutes to close them. A burning sensation hit her in the pit of her stomach as she realized that Henry was no longer next to her. She bolted upright, fearing that he'd taken off to avoid this goodbye. His humming coming from the kitchen calmed her. *I am safe, I am safe, I am safe.*

He returned with two cups of coffee and a confusingly cheery smile. "Sleep a minute there, darling?" he asked.

"Maybe a minute. What time is it?"

"Almost seven."

"Shit. I have to be on the road by eight."

"I know. Hence, coffee. I've got bread almost done. How can I help you?"

"I don't know, I think I kind of have everything together." Her physical belongings, yes. Her emotional baggage felt as if it were strewn about his cottage, hiding, unable to be scooped up and flown back home. "This feels so weird. Why are you so happy right now?"

"Ah, don't you know? I'm an eccedentesiast. I'm tricking my brain to skip the sadness."

"Not avoiding a feeling, are you Mr. Tate? I believe you told me that's bad for your health."

"Yes, of course, but just for today I'd rather not spoil my last moments with you."

She grinned. The tone had been set—no moping around for their final hour. "I'll allow it. Okay. I guess I am really leaving. I'd love some toast. And an Aperol spritz."

"Coming right up." He kissed her on the head and disappeared to the kitchen to fulfill her wants and needs, as he'd flawlessly done for the last several months. It was almost too easy.

Within the hour she found herself standing in front of his cottage in the blustery morning wind, saddled with her belongings. He'd graciously agreed to handle her affairs by returning the sewing machine and typewriter to Didier and stocked up his cottage with their combined record collection for the next guest.

She'd insisted on getting to the train station herself, as the drawn-out goodbye was just going to make it worse. Of the million things she'd wanted to say to him in this moment, she was finding it hard to formulate the words. Henry, of course, never at a loss for words, just about snapped her in half with his goodbye speech.

His hands physically held her face, metaphorically her heart.

"Go, Tess. My darling girl, I will miss you. This has been the loveliest adventure, and I think you know how hard I've fallen for you. I wouldn't change any of it. I'll be seeing you," he added through bleary eyes and the first fake smile she'd ever seen him wear. Her throat felt blocked by fallen trees from a storm, preventing any words from escaping. Instead, she buried her head in his neck and soaked up every last inch of him.

"I will miss you," was all she could squeak out, clinging to him even tighter to communicate with her body what she could not allow her mouth to say. *I love you. I hate this. I'm a mess.*

With a heaving breath, she mustered her strength to let go and pull away, turned on her heel and began walking. Tears started forming so immediately that she could not turn back to face him. Her feet carried her hurriedly, as if she might just break out into a run to overpower her heart. Seeing Henry as broken as she felt would have been too much to keep walking.

As she neared the main estate she slowed down, shaking out her limbs in an attempt to collect herself. She'd written a thank you letter to Antoinette in her very best French and planned to leave it in her door to avoid having to withstand another goodbye. As she rounded the corner to the terrace, the sight before her nearly knocked her over.

There, on the terrace, in a wrought iron chair, sat Didier, smoking a cigarette in nothing but blue checkered boxers. "*Coucou, chérie!* Time to leave so soon?" he called to her, either unwilling or unbothered to explain what he was doing there.

Full to the brim with emotion, gobsmacked by what she'd just stumbled upon and too tired to process any of it, she nodded and handed him the letter.

"Can you make sure Antoinette gets this?"

"*Bien sûr,*" he responded, suddenly solemn. He seemed to know what she'd just done in the same way she knew what he'd just done. And he was too French to address any of it. Instead, he nodded back, flicking his cigarette and rising to kiss her cheeks.

"Thank you for everything," she managed.

"*Bonne chance,*" he responded, knowing.

She pressed on, headed home.

Only it didn't feel like going home. It felt like leaving home.

November

Nineteen

Tess lay perfectly still in the creaky old bed in Maria's guest room, staring up at the jagged crack in the ceiling. She traced the crack with her eyes over and over as if expecting it to be different. But every time, from beginning to end, the crack remained unchanged. Straight, dipped down, curved up and pointing to the right. No matter what, it always ended the same.

In three hours, Tess was expected to submit a complete satirical blog post about why millennials aren't buying homes. Edgar had negotiated a consistent side gig for her at *Reductress*, and although she was grateful for the opportunity, she was finding writing to be nearly impossible.

It felt like her whole brain was flooded with Henry, with sadness, with a huge, unignorable wall of pain that also felt like a void. The tiny part of mental fortitude that needed to keep her functioning was fighting for space, but the heavy emptiness seemed incapable of receding to make room.

"Tess!" Maria yelled from the other room. The hiss of the tea kettle had been screaming for at least a full minute, but the sensational numbness prevented her brain from processing the sound. Her mother would cringe if she knew the type of houseguest she'd been.

To their credit, her dear friends had absolutely made the right call. There was nowhere in the world Tess would rather be than in Maria and Steve's cramped apartment. Even when Tess tried to decline their kind offers to host her, they were determined to care for their friend. And she needed it.

In the week since arriving back in the U.S., Tess had blown through the entire *Parks and Rec* series, a family-size tub of Nutella and only one pair of joggers. For as strong and independent as she was, she needed help.

"What do you feel?" Maria asked daily, sometimes more. Tess had become accustomed to answering this question, even if only to point to a section of the laminated feelings wheel Maria kept on the side of her fridge. Slipping swiftly into a numb abyss would have been easy—living with Maria made that impossible.

What Tess felt hung in the balance of the many shades of sad and mad. The sadness loomed when she missed Henry, recognizing his all-encompassing presence and how intricately he had been woven into the fabric of her day. She then waned into anger: at herself, for allowing this to happen in the first place and for the entanglement to become so solidified.

The sad-mad roller coaster carried her throughout her day, leaving her completely exhausted by the end. She'd had little reason to leave the apartment, and minimal responsibilities during the day, but slept each night as if she'd run a full marathon.

Her first meeting with Edgar after she settled in New York was rough. He'd been pleased with the work, and hopeful for the way the book was shaping up. However, he was clearly disappointed in Tess for her recklessness with herself.

"I need *you*, Tess. *You* are the book. Your mind, your presence, your face. You are in bad shape, *querida*, and we are running out of time for you to get yourself together." He had booked her a reading at the Strand to kick off their social media campaign to promote the new book as it neared completion. Tess was in no place to be standing in front of a crowd promoting much of anything.

Maria made Tess go on a walk with her every afternoon. When Maria had an idea, especially something that would be a good idea for you, there was no pushback allowed. She wants you to walk, you walk. She thinks you shouldn't sleep this late, and you're up. She thinks the black dress looks better, and you're wearing it. These things are not up for debate.

"Come *on*, Tess. It's getting dark and we've only walked three blocks," Maria lamented. Tess wasn't even sure her own feet were leaving the ground as she dragged on, physically behind Maria but mentally in another world. "Here's what we're going to do. You're going to do senses grounding. Then you're going to talk to me. We have twenty minutes to get home and I want to hit six more blocks. Let's go."

Aye aye, captain.

Tess rolled her eyes with her whole body, like a child being forced to eat spinach. This was her only form of protest, and Maria didn't care. Maria got her way.

"Got it out? Good. List five things you can see."

"A pushy friend. Bird shit. Orange shoes. Crusty napkin. Mountain Dew bottle."

"Great. Four things you can touch."

"Fuzzy coat. Dirty hair. Leggings. Tight ass," she added as she tapped Maria from behind. Maria unwaveringly swatted her hand and picked up speed.

"Don't be a smartass. Walk faster. Three things you can hear."

"Beeps, honks and toots!" Tess yelled out, as fast as she could. She couldn't see but was sure she had elicited Maria's smile.

"Two things you can smell."

"Sulfur. Cinnamon."

"Okay, ew. One thing you taste."

Tess contemplated this one before answering, trying to identify the odd taste in her mouth lately. It began a few days prior but had stuck.

"Kind of a weird metal sort of taste."

"Ew again. Great. Now pick up those feet, stop being an asshole and talk to me. What's coming up this week?"

Tess couldn't help but love her. Maria was so thoroughly, unapologetically herself. Tess never had to wonder if Maria liked her, and the people pleaser in her completely shut down when they were together. It was comforting to be in a friendship like that, so brutally honest that it was deeply secure.

"I have a reading on Saturday. Edgar booked me at the Strand. I'm feeling kind of nervous about it, and he is definitely nervous. I don't think he trusts me in front of humans right now. Which I kind of get."

"I would imagine. So how do you get your shit together by Saturday?"

Tess hadn't exactly considered this. She knew how she felt right now: a mess. She knew she didn't want to do the reading. But she had yet to acknowledge that none of this was permanent. That the hurt and emptiness she felt right now would of course recede in time. Even still, she could probably work on it right now to speed up the process.

"Mmm, I'm not sure. I could certainly shower. Maybe practice my passage a few times and try to sort out some answers to questions. Although Edgar usually ends up answering most questions."

"That's a weak answer." Maria shook her head as she pulled out her phone. "I'm booking you a blowout for Saturday morning. Thursday, we go find the outfit—I have the perfect boutique for you. Tonight we rehearse the passage and I'll throw some questions at you. Tomorrow night is a backup if you need more practice."

Tess marveled at her friend. Maria really could run the world.

"Deal. For real, thanks. I would be lost without you," Tess genuinely gushed, pausing her speed walk to articulate her feelings. Maria turned to face her, continuing to walk backward.

"Yes, you would, and you're about to be lost if you don't pick up the pace. I love you, dummy, let's go!" she yelled, as she turned back and continued speed-walking.

Tess held tight to her belief in the importance of community and leaning on people who truly love you.

Hours of practice, a new midnight blue jumpsuit and a full face of makeup later, Tess found herself at the Strand, feeling decently prepared.

As she looked out into the crowd, she felt both amusement and embarrassment at the consistency of the demographic at all her events. Almost exclusively female millennials who looked like they had probably spent their teenage summers at Jesus camp were seated in cheap folding chairs in front of her.

She knew them. She *was* them. Any combination of three women in the sea of Katies and Laurens and Lindsays in front of her could be teamed up to make a perfect friend group with shared interests, experiences and liberal hopes for the world.

She took a step closer to the mic, silently reciting her grounding mantra. Book readings were Tess's least favorite part of the whole writing gig. She loved writing; formulating ideas and tying them together into poetic, witty sentences exercised her favorite creative muscles.

Sharing these sentences was a whole other ball game. It was vulnerable, like she'd exposed the deepest parts of herself to the world and people were allowed—even encouraged—to review and critique her innermost thoughts. Add reading those thoughts aloud to the list while live-streaming on social media and it was almost too uncomfortable to bear.

On the bright side, readings were usually pretty positive. She'd fielded the defensive religious question or two from someone looking to dismantle her theology, but the bulk of her readers were on board with her thoughts and questions. It was a strange, quasi-celebrity feeling to talk to the people who were touched by her book. Many of them were actually very cool, and she would often strike up conversations with people she wished she could know in real life. To them, however, she wasn't real. Just a vessel leading them to the innermost workings of their own mind.

Up at the podium, Tess introduced herself, revealed the working title *Cornerstone*, and began slowly moving through the passage. Each time she began reading too fast she cleared her throat and carried on at a slower pace, breathing through each line. She felt her voice begin to pick up speed as she neared the end, desperate to cross the finish line.

"What are the things that connect my feet to the ground? The beliefs I can say out loud with no reservations? The congruence between who I am and how I seem? What is true to me?" She read the last line loudly, slowly, before giving a quick nod and stepping back from the microphone, leaving space for the applause. Relief breathed through her as she looked around, never quite sure how to look calm and confident when all eyes were on her.

"We'll take questions now," Edgar said into the microphone. This was the most stressful part, as she had already laid out her heart and soul in her writing, and questions or comments could feel so vulnerable and digging. A hand shot up immediately. Tess did her quickest body language assessment of the red-headed, tight-lipped woman and braced herself for what seemed to be coming as she stood up.

The woman smiled at the person handing her the mic and turned to face Tess. She paused, breathing so deeply that her exhale reverberated through the now-silent crowd.

"Your book killed my daughter," she said, barely moving her lips and shooting fire out of her blue eyes.

Every head in the crowd wrenched back up to face Tess, whose mouth had dropped open, agape. There was no press practice for a question like this. Edgar had also turned to Tess, mouth equally wide. Wasn't he supposed to be saving her from disasters like this?

"My daughter was a happy, married, church-going woman. Then she read your book."

Another pause, in arguably the quietest room of this many people on record.

"She left the church, left her husband and threw away her entire life. Just like you tout so proudly. Only she didn't get to go to France and start over. She became so depressed that she lost her will to live. She took her own life.

"But it feels more like you took it. What is true to you doesn't work for everyone. I don't have a question, I just needed you to know that you are responsible for what you put out into the world." She set the mic down, shuffled past the audience in her row, and headed for the door.

Tess was shaking, mouth tight with guilt and confusion and anger and sorrow. Her palms poured sweat, legs struggling to hold up the dead weight of her body which appeared to have given up. Edgar was still frozen next to her in The Quietest Room There Ever Was.

Slowly, each head in the room turned back to Tess, the alleged perpetrator of such horror. The red-headed woman had already slipped through the front door, and Tess wasn't exactly sure how, but she felt compelled to offer some sort of condolence to this person who was filled with pain and directed it at her. For god's sake, she had to say *something*.

She rolled her shoulders back, inhaled deeply and vomited in front of a live audience.

Twenty

For a million dollars Tess would not be able to recall how she got out of the Strand and down to a bench at Pier 51. Whether she walked or took a cab or was carried all the way down there, it had not registered in her mind.

She felt the cold wind on her face and the familiar sound of Edgar's humming next to her but could not register a single feeling in her body. Like the days she stayed out for way too long in the snow with her neighbor friends, completely numb to how uncomfortable she actually was. She sat for what felt like hours, waiting for the comfort of any sensation to thaw out her body and mind.

Finally, she became very aware of her stomach. It felt empty, but hot, like she'd just downed a large bowl of soup. As she analyzed this strange sensation, her body thrust her neck forward with just enough force to cover Edgar's shoes with vomit.

"Edgar, oh my god. I'm so sorry. I don't even know—I'm so sorry," she pleaded through a sea of sobs that the vomit seemed to unleash. The numbness was gone, and the feelings flooded in.

"It's okay, *querida*," he cooed, pulling her in tightly next to him. "I'm just glad you're talking. That was brutal."

"I don't even know what to say. I don't know how I feel. I just want to throw up everything inside me until I'm just a pile of skin."

He physically turned her away from him, too smart to land himself on the receiving end of her guilt bile again.

"You are traumatized. Let's get you home. What street is Maria on again?"

"That woman thinks I killed her daughter."

"You didn't. You and I both know you didn't. Tess, that was horrific. I am so sorry this happened. And that I didn't do anything about it. We can process it all later, but you're sick. Right now I just need to get you safely home."

"I'm not sick."

"Okay, love, but you are not well. Where is Maria's apartment?"

Tess breathed, considering her options. She simultaneously wanted to stand up and start sprinting and lay down and pass out. Mostly she just wanted to be alone. "She's in Chelsea. Not far. I can walk. I think I need air."

"I am not loving the idea of you walking alone in this state, Tess."

"Let me just sit another minute. I'll be okay. Walking helps me, really," she promised, throwing in a reassuring head nod for good measure. Edgar could not hide his skepticism but recognized his inability to stop her from doing whatever she wanted to do.

"Fine. But share your location with me so I can make sure you get home safe when you forget to text me that you're there."

She forced a smile. "Deal."

Edgar loved her, far beyond what was required of a close business relationship. Watching his protectiveness battle with his resolve to accept her just as she was filled Tess with such warmth. He loved her the way she needed to be loved. And she needed it.

A bit wobbly upon standing, Tess steadied herself before taking off toward home. Maria's home. Maria and Steve's home. Which she probably needed to get the hell out of to give them their space back. The feeling in her stomach grew stronger, shifting her sense of direction. She waved to Edgar, rounded the corner, and froze.

Her stomach. Memories of the bathroom floor in her old apartment, the heaving emptiness inside her, the taste in her mouth. She knew these feelings.

The only thing missing this time was the feeling of dread in the pit of her stomach. Instead, she snapped into action.

Tess needed to get to a drugstore. Putting one foot in front of the other, she took off.

Navigating New York at this time of year was especially difficult with lingering Thanksgiving visitors and curated Christmas displays popping up in every window. Winding through packs of other humans was never something Tess excelled at in her innate passivity, but today she was on a mission.

She snaked through happy couples, driven businesspeople, loud families from out of town. With each step, she picked up her pace, now with a wild excitement to confirm what her body already seemed to be telling her.

Just once she paused, willing her esophagus to keep down whatever was left of the contents of her stomach.

One more block and the familiar red signage appeared. She hurried through the door to the drug store around the corner from Maria's just as a middle-aged man in a camel hair coat was coming out. He had to step to the side, pick a lane to keep from colliding. Walking on autopilot, she neglected to smile cheerfully and profusely thank the man for the decency of not plowing through her.

"You're welcome," he yelled back at her, as if moving from the center of a two-way walkway deserved a Nobel prize.

The Tess of the last thirty years would have laid awake at night thinking through this interaction, and how she should have thanked him, or at least smiled. The Tess of today had just been ripped to shreds emotionally, professionally, mentally and physically. An entitled middle-aged man was powerless against the events of the day thus far, and the physical shift she felt inside her being. She pressed on, unbothered, set on completing her drugstore purchase before Edgar would check her location.

The rest of the walk home resembled a scene from season one of *Sex and the City* where Carrie floated home from a successful date. Tess was certainly walking, but seemingly on air. This ability to remove her brain from its obsession with control and allow her body to take over was one of the most important practices she'd brought home from France. Family rule number one stuck: let it go.

Finally, at the door of Maria's apartment, Tess was out of breath and fumbled with her keys. The telltale sign of urgency is the inability to remember which key—the one used upwards of ten times a day—unlocks the door. She finally made it inside and beelined for the bathroom.

The quickness with which her feet carried her across the cold hardwood to the ceramic tile was almost amusing, drastically different from her experience in her old apartment when she was previously in this position. The last time she dragged it out for days, finding any minuscule task extraordinarily important to avoid the inevitable. But now she was hopeful, almost cheery. Desperate to decode what her body was telling her.

There's nothing like anxious excitement to prevent a body from working properly. As she sat on the toilet, grasping the stick between her legs, Tess took stock of her body. Her shoulders were tense, she was holding her breath and her organs felt like they wanted to jump out of her throat. She inhaled, repeated *I'm safe*, and promptly soaked her hand in urine.

Tess had taken dozens of pregnancy tests in her life. She knew exactly what two minutes felt like. Her brain had traced a familiar cycle of hope and dread and dreams and what-ifs. She sat and waited for the same feelings to inevitably come—but they didn't.

Before Tess could overanalyze the difference in her mindset waiting for this test, her phone buzzed. Her breath caught, blood rushing to her head as she read Henry's name next to the message:

Hi. I'm recording at the studio. It's snowing. Can we talk next week?

Exchanging numbers before leaving France was so odd, and they hadn't exactly decided what the protocol would be for communication. For two weeks she'd picked up her phone, set it back down, and repeated the cycle, trying to determine what to say. A text too soon and they'd pick up right where they left off. Wait too long and it becomes too much pressure. She had typed out dozens of texts of varying degrees of weight and sent none.

And yet—unaware of how much she wanted to just tell him everything—he was there. As if the piece of her heart he held in his had alerted him to how much she needed him right now.

Without a second thought, she texted back: *J'adore la neige.* She quickly added: *Love to talk.*

His three little bubbles came up. Knowing he was there, somewhere, typing back to her while she was here, mentally with him, sparked a light in her chest that felt like hope.

A picture of a thin layer of snow covering the street outside his window came through with a simple message: *I'll call you.*

Tess double-tapped to heart the picture and the text, breaking into a smile so wide the confines of her cheeks could barely contain it. The possibility that Henry was somewhere cheesy smiling at his phone too only pushed the limit of her jaw.

She set her phone down on the counter, only aware that she had knocked something off by the sound of plastic bouncing on the tile floor.

Still in her Henry stupor, Tess reached down to pick it up and froze, remembering the reason she was sitting in this bathroom. The plastic so light in her hands for the weight of what it held. She slowly spun the blue and white stick to reveal her answer.

Two blue lines.

December

Twenty-one

For four days straight Tess tiptoed around Maria's apartment and down the streets of Manhattan as if she were carrying a hundred-year-old Fabergé egg intended for the king of Spain.

It had taken over an hour for her to set the test down and leave the bathroom that day, only slipping out when she heard Maria come home.

"Why are you walking like that?" Maria had asked, immediately noticing the shift in her gait.

Unable to lie to her best friend Tess collapsed on the sofa and spilled all of it—the book reading, the text from Henry, the positive test. Maria listened intently, squeezing Tess's hand through the difficult parts and letting her shed every tear her body could produce. Tess found the words rolled out of her mouth easily, like her tongue had retired from playing defense against releasing true, raw emotions.

"I feel like I'm lying naked in the middle of the street in the fetal position. Like I've been stripped down to nothing but I'm clutching my own body to protect this thing inside me like not one single other thing matters. As if it's the only thing that is important."

Maria nodded slowly, processing. Her face softened as she considered how to pose the question that needed to be asked.

"So, you're having this baby?"

Tess sat back, first surprised that Maria had asked the question, and then more surprised that she had not even asked *herself* the question. Even in its legitimacy, it stung a little.

She knew her options—she'd been down this road before and was thankful to live in a state where she had the autonomy to choose. But not for a second did she consider not having *this* baby. Everything about this felt so different.

"I know it sounds crazy. I have no idea how I'm going to do this. But I am going to do this." Instead of leaning into the details, of holding Tess accountable in the lovingly firm way she usually did, Maria wrapped her up in her arms. They cried together on the sofa, letting out intermittent soft laughs, until Steve walked through the door. The three of them had a celebratory dinner together that night of plain potatoes to accommodate Tess's nausea.

Jo was overwhelmingly enthusiastic. She and Liz had decided against kids, but there was an obvious part of her that seemed to be suppressing the desire to be a parent. Instead, she projected it onto Tess.

"Liz can make a crib, like a good sturdy one. You can stay with us as long as you want. My sister has just buckets of hand-me-down clothes. We can get you everything you need. Oh my god, Tess, I can't even believe it. I am SO excited for you!" The shoddy service during their FaceTime call hid Tess's slightly glazed-over eyes from absorbing Jo's enthusiasm. Upon hanging up, she immediately vomited.

So far the vomiting was bothersome, but not terrible. The constant state of nausea and not knowing if or when she would throw up was worse. Tess sucked on ginger candies nearly constantly throughout the day just to manage. Maria had booked her an urgent OB-GYN appointment for the next week, which Tess hoped would provide some advice on how to manage these symptoms and continue to live her life.

Reality began to settle into Tess's psyche after five days of knowing she was pregnant. Rushing to meet Edgar for coffee she threw on a knit sweater and pulled her jeans up over her slightly bloated belly.

From the outside, she probably looked exactly the same, but she *felt* bigger. Fuller. Like anyone who saw her would instantly know. A green beanie and a red lip and she was out the door, hoping her face would distract from her body she was sure would give her away.

Edgar sat in the middle of the community table at Bean & Bean. Unlike Tess, who would have opted for a tiny two-seater, he liked to be in the mix, bumping elbows and exchanging energy with interesting strangers. A smile crept across Tess's lips, admiring Edgar for being exactly himself.

Edgar waved. Tess box breathed as she made her way over to him. *I can do this.*

"*Querida, ¿qué pasa?*" he asked, planting a kiss on each cheek.

"I'm okay. I'm feeling strong," she managed with a contradictory weak smile. She was telling the truth—an emergency therapy session with Jenny and thorough debriefing with her friends had led her through processing most of her feelings about what happened at the Strand. The tiny seed in her belly was now at the forefront of her mind.

"Well, I like strong. You certainly look much better than the last time I saw you. Different," he mused, his gaze lingering on hers.

There was no actual question there, but it felt like Edgar had opened a window for her to elaborate. Instead, she slammed it shut and drew the curtains closed with business.

"So, what do we do?" she asked.

Edgar snapped out of friend mode and back into work mode. "Well, we were live streaming on Instagram, so we definitely have to address it. We've put together a statement about the incident for you to share on social media. It's pretty simple, but we felt you shouldn't go too much into it. I wanted you to acknowledge the woman's pain without taking responsibility for the tragedy. What do you think?" he asked, pulling up his notes app.

Tess scanned the three sentences written for her, finishing with the makeshift social media signature Edgar had created. It was certainly simple, which she didn't mind. But part of the story seemed to be missing.

"May I?" she asked, glancing up at Edgar. He waved his hand, offering the go-ahead. One more sentence before her signature poured out of her fingers furiously. The new statement read:

I want to address an audience member at my most recent book reading at the Strand. I am so sorry for your loss. My hope for anyone reading my books is to feel free to live their truest self. My deeper hope for the world is that it would be a safe place for everyone to do so. XX Tess

She set the phone back down and pushed it toward Edgar, feeling a lump creep up higher in her throat, harder to push down. He quickly read the addition, nodding.

"This sounds like you," he agreed.

"Edgar, I believe it," Tess said as her emotions heightened. "I actually mean all of this. I feel for this woman—really, I do. But I don't feel personally responsible. I know I didn't do this, and I know I can't fix this for her," she continued, now smiling through tears. The hormonal toing and froing was exhausting, feeling like she was out in the ocean, jumping over and ducking under huge waves that threatened to knock her right over.

"That's true. I'm glad you know that. But you feel...sad...and?" he asked, searching her face for answers.

A laugh escaped her as she wiped a tear away. "Relieved, maybe? I feel a peace about the whole situation that I didn't think I would feel. And that just makes me feel grateful. An earlier version of myself would have been sick with responsibility and humiliation and sadness. Instead, I feel peace. So, I guess I just have a lot of feelings and they're all coming out at once." She picked up her green tea, sipping between smiles and tears. So full she could burst.

"Tess, honey, I am proud of you. I think we should move forward as planned with the release. It seems like you're in a good place—and coming here today I wasn't sure the shape you'd be in. So, we'll go ahead and post and move forward with the social media campaign."

Tess was beaming. She let everything pour out of her, holding nothing back. *Nothing*. Without warning she bent down and vomited—for the second time—right onto Edgar's oxfords.

His eyes widened so large they rivaled the giant teacup sitting between them.

"Oh my god. I am so sorry—I can't believe I—not again..." Tess ducked under the table to clean up the mess, too pale to flush amid her embarrassment.

When she sat back up to face him—still frozen in his seat—his eyes had narrowed, quizzically.

"Tess..." he began. She watched his wheels turning, saw the spark of revelation appear in his face. He knew.

She nodded, semi-relieved.

Edgar's head dropped to his chest, sending alarm through Tess's whole body. For a second he paused, before lifting his chin back up to her to reveal the widest grin she'd ever seen on his familiar face.

"*Querida*," he breathed, clamoring out of his seat and full-on running around the community table to pull her into a deep, multi-minute hug.

Tess held tight. She needed this.

Regardless of an actual bloodline relation, Tess received family approval.

Henry finally texted again to say he would be calling in the morning, but that service was not strong enough to FaceTime. The air in Tess's lungs gushed out in relief—she wasn't sure she was ready to face him yet. The whole ordeal felt so clinical and business-like. Worlds away from the effortless communication they had enjoyed in the less-real world.

Tess was going to have to deliver arguably the most important news of either of their lives via their first phone call, ever.

Maria, Steve, Tess and Jo via FaceTime sat at the kitchen table to devise a script for delivery. Telling him was not a question—Tess had learned her lesson with Jake. *How* to tell him was the tricky part. It was still so early, the details so complicated, and there was no future plan to reveal to him. They had carefully avoided commandeering each other's lives and dreams already. This news had the power to overtake both of their futures.

All this considered—the pregnancy reveal roundtable was nowhere near settling on a plan for how to navigate this.

"I think just say it. Don't come at it with any plans or ways you see him involved or not involved. If it doesn't feel like it's his choice, he's going to feel trapped," Steve said.

"Ew, fuck that," Maria retorted in all her feminist glory, clearly put off by her partner. "He's not the one with the human growing inside him. If anyone is trapped it's Tess—I mean, I know you're not trapped. But seriously, fuck his implicit right to his individuality and choices. Tess is the one sacrificing her body and her future."

"No, but I do have a choice. I'm choosing to have the baby, so I really do want him to feel like he has a choice—"

"Guys I can't hear—" poor Jo yelled through the phone, desperate to be involved.

"I mean, legally he'll be required to pay child support. And we know he has the money," Maria continued, ignoring Jo's plea.

"I'm not going to talk to him about child support yet. I just want him to know. I want him to know I'm actually excited, and that I don't expect anything from him. I just want to inform him. And I want him to take some time and process all of it before we talk about any details."

"Yeah, I think that's a good approach. Give him the info. It's not like this will be your last conversation about it. Men need time to process so we don't say our dumbass first instinctual response," Steve said, attempting to redeem himself.

"I know that's right," Maria shot back, sending Steve a killer look.

"Okay cool, so I'll see you next week!" Jo interrupted, clearly annoyed at her outsider treatment but trying to sound cheerful to be a part of this.

"Can't wait. Love you, Jo." Tess was genuinely excited to head to Portland for part two of her "friends as family" tour of the northeast, but the current dilemma took precedence.

Conversation-rehearsing in between repeated dreams of swimming alone in the middle of the ocean kept Tess mostly awake for the entire night. She had optimistically set her alarm as if she would need any help waking up. Once she finally dropped the hope of rest, she hobbled into the kitchen to work on her transition out of half-sleep and into the day.

Aside from the nausea, ditching coffee was the hardest part of pregnancy. Although online forums (which Tess perused daily) assured her that a cup of coffee in the morning would do no harm, she was still in the "too good to believe" stage of pregnancy processing and had swapped her coffee for green tea. The only problem was that, of course, green tea doesn't do shit when you don't sleep.

The plan had been to meditate for half an hour, drink her tea and see if she could keep a bagel down before Henry's call. Plans be damned, Tess found herself unable to sit still, and ventured out into the early December cold, leaning into distraction over meditation. Cold made her feel alive, grounded her. Today she needed to be as calm and grounded as she possibly could.

As she walked around the block, she glanced at each face she passed. Being pregnant felt so monumental and life-changing. She felt like yelling "I am with child!" at every person walking by, as if news this big in her own life should be life-changing for everyone else as well. Yet strangers passed by looking as bored, worried and busy as ever with no acknowledgment of passing a person growing another actual person. *Pregnancy is so weird.*

Back at Maria's apartment, Tess had just enough time to push a plain bagel down her throat. Every minute that ticked closer to nine o'clock seemed to double her heart rate. Right on time—which felt like an 'I love you' in and of itself—Henry's call came through.

"Hi," she answered, feigning calm as if this was any normal call.

"Hello there. Wow, it's good to hear your voice." God, she missed that accent.

"It's good to hear you too. This feels a little…"

"Weird?'

"Yeah, I guess—maybe just normal. And we're not normal," she pointed out.

"No, we're not. I suppose we'll have to pretend, then. How are you, darling?"

Henry and Tess—not the Henry and Tess pair of Abzac who spent every second together, but a Henry and a Tess of the real world—caught up. The need to catch up, even the act of talking on the phone was so foreign to their relationship.

She told him about New York, Edgar, Maria and Steve, even the Strand. He told her about recording, a disagreement with his manager, and how he'd been spending some time with his family. Her heart soared when he disclosed that he'd told them all about her, and they wanted to meet her. She remained grounded by the nausea her ginger chew was just barely keeping at bay, and the thought of how the hell she was going to gear this light, catch-up conversation toward "we're having a baby."

"You know, catching up with you feels so odd. Wrong, sort of. Like we shouldn't need to catch up," he said.

"Ha. I know what you mean. But this is what we agreed on, I guess."

Agreed was not the right word. Technically they had not agreed on this, they just couldn't agree on something other than this. He graciously remained silent about that.

"Well, I've had a bit of a change of plans. I'm actually not in London right now."

"Oh yeah? Where are you?" Her heart pounded, jumping to far too optimistic conclusions.

"Halifax. Aunt Rita has been sick and needed someone to come tend to the house while she's in hospital. I finished recording and came right away. She should be back home in a few days, and then I'll need to stay with her a bit until she can be on her own again. I don't have an exact timeline, but I will surely be here through Christmas."

"So, you're saying we're on the same continent?"

She could hear his smile through the phone. "I'm saying we're on the same continent. Not exactly close by, but just a time zone off. How long are you going to be in New York?"

"I leave Sunday. I'm going up to Portland to be with Jo and Liz for a few weeks for the holidays."

"And then what?"

She audibly let out a whoosh of air. "I'm not sure, really."

"Tess, I want to see you."

He put it so plainly, laid out exactly what he wanted. His directness made her feel safe, secure, not having to guess what was going on or how he felt.

"I want to see you, too," she responded. She meant it. Her body longed to touch his, to be held by *him* in her fragile state. Like being with him would keep the baby more secure, to help it grow into an actual human. In case she didn't have the strength to do it all on her own.

"Come to Halifax. Meet Aunt Rita. Let me make a Christmas lamb for you. You have to see the sunrise."

Her mind raced with logistics, but her heart was stronger. She couldn't imagine seeing him again like this, but she couldn't imagine staying away from him either. This would be a better way to tell him, she reasoned.

"Okay. I'll come," she agreed, immediately feeling lighter than she had in a month.

The busyness of her final days in New York kept Tess from obsessing over the impending Henry reunion. After their conversation, she called Jo to sort out plans. She and Liz had booked a house in Bar Harbor for Christmas, so Tess would take the ferry to Yarmouth on the twenty-first to visit Henry for a night.

Pregnancy exhaustion worked in her favor, and even though her extensive traveling plans had wrenched her anxiety up to the max, she routinely passed out every night by 8 pm.

The OB-GYN appointment Maria had made for her was so strange Tess couldn't believe it was real. Tess had shown up, stripped down, done some bloodwork and received a five-page packet about pregnancy, copyrighted in 1997. She was estimated to be seven weeks pregnant. The whole ordeal was so routine, so clinical for something that felt like once-in-a-lifetime magic.

As the doctor calmly explained what to expect Tess felt like yelling "I'm making a PERSON in here!! How are you acting so normal and sending me out in the world to just *live* right now??" Apparently, having a child is as routine and normal as life gets. She vowed to look for a more holistic midwifery practice in Portland for her next appointment.

For her final night in New York, Maria made (ordered) dinner for them and invited Edgar and his husband Jeff to join. If everyone hadn't already known Tess was pregnant, this dinner would easily have given it away. Tears continually regenerated in her eyes for the entire evening, occasionally rolling down her cheeks. All she could stomach was plain rice and honeydew—the tiny summer baby inside her seemed to want melons all the time.

As if Tess didn't know herself at all, she decided to make a toast.

"I don't know what to say," she started, heaving a large sob. "This last month has been...I mean I would be nowhere without you guys. You're my chosen family and have loved me better than my own flesh and blood. None of you have to be here. And I don't know why you chose me, but I am so deeply grateful. So, thanks for loving me, I guess. There is nothing I want that I don't already have," she promised, the classic line her heart believed when everything felt right. She cheersed her tea with everyone's champagne glasses, laugh-crying at how much she meant every word she said.

"We love you, Tessie. And we love this new baby, and this new book. We are here for all of it and could not be more proud of you," Maria said, once again unleashing whatever thin dam was holding back the rest of Tess's tears.

She looked around the table, immensely grateful to herself for letting go and to these people for catching her. Her cornerstones.

Twenty-two

A visceral sense of déjà vu washed over Tess as she stared out of the train window, heading north for Portland.

She was eight years old, boarding the marketed "Polar Express" with her family. The old steam engine drove a two-hour loop up to Pennsylvania and back, stopping for quick pictures with Santa.

She could still see Luke and little Rachel's excited faces pressed up against the window, cheeks pink from the cold. Her parents held hands sitting in the seat across from the kids—the only memory of visible affection Tess could recall between them. A warm glow vignetted the memory: all five of them smushed into the train booth, full of giggles and hot chocolate and youthful joy.

Reconciling the warmth of family memories and the cold Tess now felt toward them left her feeling lukewarm. A pang of longing for the warmth again struck her hard. For a long, genuine mom hug. To giggle with Luke and Rachel. To hear her dad affectionately call her "kid", even in adulthood.

The snow on the evergreens whizzing by outside still conjured the same joy inside her as it always did. A true snow-lover, Tess spent most of her childhood winters with a spoon under her pillow and her pajamas inside out and backward in hopes of a snow day. When it came, she was outside every minute she could be, sometimes just sitting silently as it fell on her. As cold as it was, snow made her feel warm inside.

As cold as her family was to her, maybe she could make space for warmth for them, too.

A sudden onslaught of nausea had her scrambling for the trusty saltine crackers she kept in her bag at all times. She'd gotten better at managing her nausea. The OB-GYN hadn't provided much relief, dismissing it as one of those things women just deal with in pregnancy while continuing to live their lives.

Tess could not imagine how someone with a normal job in an office could handle constant nausea and random vomiting throughout the day. The condition seemed poorly named as "morning sickness" when it tended to worsen in the afternoon and evening. She tried to breathe through it, taking tiny sips of water and snacking on crackers, distracting her body from the discomfort. With nothing to do on the train, the nausea was creeping back up, and she needed her brain to focus on something else.

Since the first pregnancy test, Tess had been consumed by what she felt about the pregnancy. She was excited, nauseous, nervous, thrilled to be forever connected to Henry in this way. The thing about pregnancy is that it often results in a baby. The progression of this, the eventual actual human *baby* part of the whole ordeal had barely crossed her mind.

What would she name this thing?

Louise?

Bowen?

Birdie?

She hadn't even considered whether it would be a boy or a girl.

When and how would she tell her family? *Oof.* She would come back to this one later.

Where would she and the baby live? The northeast was certain, she needed to be close enough to Maria and Jo, and Edgar for work. She'd be comfortable enough in a one-bedroom with just a little baby. Right? Did babies need their own room? *Come back to that one, too.*

The finances were a concern, of course, but Tess was raised on frugal practicality and an inclination to save.

Would she breastfeed?

What kind of diapers would she use?

Did she want an unmedicated birth?

Who would watch the babe when she had meetings?

Could you have a baby without family?

Her anxiety spiral was cut off by the loudspeaker. "Next stop, Portland." Tess gulped and steadied herself before collecting her bags. These questions would have to wait until she had a trusted sounding board to process with. Ideally, someone who knew anything about parenthood.

Jo was immediately visible upon arrival—not just to Tess, but to everyone on the train. She was jumping up and down, holding a sparkly sign that said "Welcome, Mama!" in puffy-painted bubble letters. This was certainly not the subtlety Tess had requested, but Jo was who she was. Liz stood six feet away sucking on her weed pen, clearly as mortified by the fanfare as Tess felt. Jo's jumping and shouting only got louder as the passengers shuffled off the train.

Tess chose to be touched rather than embarrassed, plastered on a smile and hurried off to meet her friends and begin her month in Maine.

Living with Liz and Jo was a stark contrast to living with Maria and Steve. It seemed that at least one of them was there *all the time*, even though they both worked outside of the house. Jo ran a successful construction company but preferred working from home in between site visits as opposed to the fancy office she paid for each month. Liz, a graphic designer, went to her office every morning but came home at lunch to play with their dog, Loafer. Most days she couldn't bring herself to leave the Loaf again and wound up finishing work from home.

The accommodations were certainly preferable to New York. Jo and Liz's townhouse was twice the size of Maria's apartment, and Tess had her own large room she retreated to often in need of alone time. Liz cooked *Bon Appetit* recipes each night, catering to Tess's wild pregnancy whims and nausea triggers. For a week straight they had some form of potatoes with every single meal which is, of course, what the menu probably looks like in heaven.

The majority of Tess's writing happened seated in the bay window of the guest room, looking out down the cobblestone street, grateful for the view. Portland had a heartwarming charm that New York could only dream of manufacturing. But New York had the people, and Portland looked like a walking L.L.Bean catalog casting call without a shred of diversity.

Itching to get out of the house, Tess found a coffee shop to frequent for her morning tea. Snow was almost a daily occurrence, and never had a break enough to melt. She pulled on her boots each day and zipped up her giant puffer jacket, eventually bringing her laptop to not have to head back out in the cold with her tea.

Sitting by the window of the shop, she imagined what it would be like to live here, down the street from her friends, in this cold, charming town that felt just slightly too cool for her. It didn't "click" perfectly in her mind—but it could certainly work.

Jo was almost too eager to take care of Tess. Multiple times a day she asked her how she was feeling, what she needed, if she was okay. While preferable to the silence Tess would have experienced if she'd been on her own right now, she had to temper the stifling excitement.

"Jo. I love you. I'm good. I'll let you know if I'm not good." It was much easier to reject Jo's involvement than Maria's.

She had to imagine this was similar to the experience she would have had if she lived close to her own mother. Her mother, who still did not know she was pregnant. Who would become a grandmother without her knowledge, unless Tess worked up the courage to tell her.

On a brisk walk back from the coffee shop one day, she found the energy to return a call from Luke, slightly panicking when he answered rather than let it go to voicemail. Their phone conversations were typically brief but served as the only updates she could give to and receive from her family.

He knew she was in Portland, and that her new book was coming out soon. He relayed that their parents had been bickering a lot lately and that their dad seemed to be getting forgetful. Tess wondered if they had heard about the debacle at the Strand but chickened out of asking. Luke told her Rachel had a boyfriend and they had gotten serious really quickly. She debated texting Rachel but bailed with no idea what the follow-up would have looked like. Soon, Rachel would likely be engaged. And Tess would likely not be invited to the wedding.

She could not bring herself to give Luke the biggest news. Not yet.

The omission made Tess uneasy. She was no stranger to the consequences of not sharing updates with people who deserved to know, people whose lives would also be affected by her news.

On the other hand, if you've disowned your daughter or sister, it seemed unfair that you'd get to claim a grandchild or niece or nephew.

She resolved to tell Luke once there was more information and a set plan he could pass on to the others who would have nothing but questions. Then it would be in their hands to reach out. It was the best she could do with what she had, but the gaping hole of her absent family throughout pregnancy so far and in how she imagined parenthood was as hard to ignore as her nausea.

Tess convinced herself with waning confidence that the next time she called Luke, she'd be ready.

A week into her Portland stay, Tess sat alone writing at the kitchen table, racing against a blog post deadline. Liz had just returned from her walk with the Loaf and uncharacteristically joined her at the table. Tess loved Liz for her quiet, calm presence, but rarely sat down and had a conversation with her. Liz shined in muttering quick-witted comments under her breath, and Tess bet that if she said what she thought out loud more often she may be the funniest person anyone knew.

"It's so fucking cold," Liz muttered, half to Tess and half to herself.

"I don't mind it. I'd love to live in the cold."

"Where are you going to live, anyway?" Surprising engagement from Liz, but a very good, blunt question.

"Honestly, I don't know. I'm lucky that I have decent flexibility with my job. But I'm realizing more and more that I'm going to need help with this baby, and I don't know how to do that without family nearby."

"You know you have us. I mean for real. We're not having kids, and that's a concession Jo made for me. But she'd love to be Auntie

Weirdo to your kid. Portland isn't exactly the most affordable place to live, but we would be happy to help make it all work for you. Like seriously." Liz's eye contact was so intense, so unorthodox that Tess had to look away. The sincerity was burning into her retinas.

"Thanks, Liz. For real. I'm considering it, honestly. I really haven't thought about it thoroughly yet. I still have a while before I know if this is really happening. I mean it is, but it's still very delicate."

Liz furrowed her brow, considering this information. Tess hadn't really considered this much either, that such a large percentage of pregnancies end in miscarriage. It felt so solid to her, even from the beginning. Her body and mind knew it even before she took the test, and the fear that this wouldn't actually come to fruition hadn't fully reared its ugly head in her outcome spiral. She knew she was pregnant. She knew she was having a baby. Even if it was still a bit too early to feel this sure.

Liz thrust her chin down in a quick nod before walking away.

The coffee shop down the street was becoming Tess's office more each day. She was finally able to get back into the groove of writing at normal times and treating her workday like a nine-to-five. This was easier away from Liz and Jo's house, and she'd cozied up to a barista she thought could be a real friend.

"Five minutes, Tess," her new friend Torie called over the counter. The only negative to the place was its 3 pm closing time.

"Mmhmm," Tess replied without looking up. She was on a roll with draft number five, rewriting a substantial section of chapter seventeen that Edgar had ripped to shreds, and didn't want to lose her steam. She only had two days until they left for Bar Harbor, and she had already resigned to not work over her self-declared Christmas break.

After the shortest five minutes of her life, Torie appeared in the chair across from Tess.

"Time's up, buttercup," she said with a coy smile. Torie had the type of charm that had strangers fall in love with her after a thirty-second interaction. She seemed incapable of not flirting with people.

Tess continued typing just to the end of her sentence before glancing back up at Torie. "There. Done. I'll get out of your hair now."

"Not so fast. I've decided that since I've become such a crucial part of whatever the hell you're always writing about, I should get to read some of it. Can I?"

Tess considered this. She and Edgar were inching incredibly close to the final draft deadline, edging toward it and pulling back in a dance of "it's done" and "one more thing". She figured it wouldn't hurt to get another set of eyes on it.

"Fine," she said, giving in. "But it's not done."

Torie swung her seat around to Tess's side, so close that Tess was practically pinned between her and the window.

"It's kind of a how-to book. I wrote my first book about breaking down belief systems and questioning societal structures. This one is about how to build them back up without losing yourself. Or at least what has worked for me."

Torie studied Tess's face as she was talking as if she were the most interesting person on earth. God, she was good.

She began reading intently. Several "mmm" and "hah"s escaped her as she blazed through the chapter. Whether she was enjoying it or not wasn't clear, but at least she was reacting.

"Shit, this is good. Important," she finally said, raising her head back up from the computer. "You are something else."

Tess hadn't realized how close Torie had been leaning over her to read. Now their faces were just inches apart. Torie smelled of amber and tiny freckles Tess had never noticed danced across her nose and cheeks as if they'd just popped up. The proximity was intense, but Tess fought the urge to draw back.

Torie smiled wide, as if reading Tess's mind, totally amused by her desperation to assess the friendliness versus flirtiness of the situation. Before Tess settled into one camp, Torie leaned in and kissed her.

The familiar adrenaline rush sparked at her lips and rushed down to her toes. She'd only kissed girls in middle school when her group of friends used each other to practice before kissing boys. There had never been anything romantic or even particularly sexual about it, just pure research. This was new to Tess.

It didn't last long, and after Torie pulled away she walked back to the coffee bar and continued working as if nothing happened. Tess sat, stunned, relishing in the excitement of this new experience. When her brain finally connected back to her body, she packed up her computer, gave Torie an awkward wave and headed out the door.

"See you later, Tess," Torie called in her low voice, which now sounded decidedly sultry. So much for making a new friend in Portland.

Tess walked home, mind flooded with the new information she'd learned about herself: real Tess was a little bit gay.

Twenty-three

Tess hadn't told anyone about her interaction with Torie and hadn't really had the time to process it herself. In part she was relieved—maybe this wasn't a life-changing, identity-shaping revelation. Maybe it didn't have to mean so damn much. Maybe she had achieved her goal of just living her life, doing what she wanted and not stressing so much over the labels.

The women packed Jo's Subaru to the brim for their five-day trip to the island of Bar Harbor. To their credit, it was forecasted to be absolutely freezing, and they were lugging enough Christmas decorations to cover their entire Airbnb.

"Honey, please, just let me do it," Jo offered to Liz who was repacking the trunk for the third time. Liz took a long hit off her weed pen, ignoring Jo completely, and began rearranging bags again. Jo rolled her eyes and gave up, throwing her attention elsewhere.

"How are you feeling, Tessie? One more day until you see him," she asked, faking lightheartedness when she was so clearly still annoyed.

"Um. Good? I really don't know what to expect. I am excited to see him. I miss him a lot. I'm definitely nervous about this whole conversation we have to have. And about the aftermath of what seeing him will do to me. But overall, I guess mostly excited." A loud grunt from Liz took the attention off Tess and her half-honest answer.

She *was* excited. She wanted to see him, she even wanted to tell him about the baby. What she didn't want was to acknowledge how strongly this could affect her.

She didn't want to think about the day after seeing him, and how it might feel to have to wake up again from another Henry hangover. She wasn't sure Jo really knew how hard she could fall off the high of being with him again, and she was purposefully avoiding considering whether it would be worth it or not. So she settled on excited until she had to face the consequences.

The car ride was longer than they'd expected with holiday traffic, but Tess slept through almost the whole thing. She'd never in her life been as tired as she was in pregnancy. Even with nine hours of sleep each night, she found herself unable to make it through a day without napping.

The online forums confirmed that the second trimester might provide some reprieve, but that the third trimester (and pretty much all of parenting) would be equally as exhausting. So, buckle up, buttercup! There was a lot of this type of negative, "just you wait" rhetoric on American pregnancy sites. She found that Mumsnet was a better fit for realistic expectations without the doom and gloom of becoming a mother.

A mother.

There were so many stages to wrapping her mind around pregnancy that Tess had barely scratched the surface of the ways this may change her own identity. She logically understood the birth part. The real-life baby. The body changes. The shift in daily routine. But the all-encompassing identity change was out of her realm of comprehension.

For someone so freshly comfortable in her own skin, this upset to the delicate balance of the person she had found herself to be was scary. She had no way of knowing how she'd react, the kind of mom she would be. The lack of control she would have not only over herself but the entire life of another person.

Tess could feasibly work from the example her mom had set in her own parenting, adding and deleting parts to make it work. There would be shifts, of course, to unconditional love and encouraging kids to make their own choices. She could replicate the care her mom showed her, some of the selflessness, and instilling the importance of loving others. Add in a bit more independence, fun and open-mindedness. A lot more silliness and break from rigidity.

This could work—Tess would be the parent she wished she had. If nothing else, she certainly knew what it looked like to parent without much more from a partner than sperm and some financial stability.

"Next left and it's the house at the end of the road," she heard Jo tell Liz, just as Tess was trying to picture herself in her own version of mom clothes. As if her outfit would give her insight into the type of parent she'd be.

The forest green cabin was bigger than Tess had been expecting for just the three of them. They had foregone Christmas presents for each other this year and thrown the money into renting a place more extravagant than the budget-friendly traveling they were used to.

Jo had to be on the waterfront. Liz wanted at least three bedrooms in case she couldn't stand Jo's snoring. Tess requested a working fireplace. They settled on a charming A-frame with expansive views of Frenchman Bay, with a front window magnificent enough to justify the degree to which they'd exceeded their budget. Tess was immediately transported to Cap-Ferret, and the way her breath caught at the view from the bungalow she and Henry had shared. It was awe, his favorite feeling.

"Dinner in twenty!" Jo called up the steps as Tess was unpacking. A pile of colorful sweaters covered her bed, mixed with a few pairs of leggings. Zipped pants were out of the question at this point in pregnancy. She was putting off the full plunge into maternity clothes, planning to stretch her leggings collection to its limit first.

A chunky emerald sweater dress was the only piece she actually hung up in the closet. This was for Henry, also coupled with leggings and her vintage green plaid duster coat. She'd accessorize with Doc Martens and a grey beanie to appear to not be trying too hard.

She didn't know winter Henry, and he didn't know winter Tess. She'd been more clear on the outfit she'd wear to see him than the words she'd planned to tell him he was going to be a father. Priorities.

Dinner with Jo and Liz was short, the tension from the stress of traveling still clinging to everyone. Tess claimed nausea and exhaustion and excused herself from having to endure any more passive aggression. Besides, she had one of the biggest days of her life ahead of her.

Without the aid of CBD salve and melatonin supplements, Tess found herself as far from sleep as she could be. She used the hours to rehearse the perfect way to tell Henry about the baby. To convey excitement. Relieve pressure from him to respond. To be sure, above all else, that he knew she wanted this because *she* actually wanted this. And, if she couldn't quite get the words out, she'd bring the pregnancy test to speak for her.

Finally, she drifted off, repeating the line over and over that she fully believed in her heart: *we made magic.*

The ferry from Bar Harbor to Yarmouth was a solid three and a half hours. Pregnancy nausea and boats don't mix, and Tess spent the majority of the trip clutching a surprisingly clean porcelain toilet, praying for it to be over. *I am safe. I am safe. I am safe.* This would certainly be a miserable trip back, in more ways than one.

When the port was clearly in sight, Tess caught herself in a natural, but deliberate, box breath pattern. He was there, somewhere, no longer separated by thousands of miles. Soon enough, she would see him. Hear him. Touch him. The weeks she'd spent longing for more time with him would be in the rear-view mirror. For now, he'd be hers again.

Fighting a war against the anxiety welling up in her lungs, she fumbled her phone out of her pocket and texted Jo and Maria.

I am almost here. I'm freaking out.

Sometimes, just saying it, just sending the real feelings out to people who cared about you was enough to temper them.

You got this, Maria responded, immediately.

We love you, Jo followed. Her people. Her family. Always there when she needed them, as if the three of them were made from the same cloth.

She threw up, just one more time for good measure, and made her way off the boat.

Henry and Tess had texted briefly, organizing, confirming the details of a trip that made no actual logical sense. She'd be traveling seven hours just to stay for a night and then do the whole trip in reverse. She wondered if he knew there was something serious, some reason she would come all this way to see him for such a short time.

Once on land again she steadied her sea legs, if only temporarily. She scanned the crowd of travelers and loved ones at the port.

As soon as he caught her eye, the trip didn't matter. She would have done anything to be here, now, with him.

Tess felt like she'd walked into a sliding glass door she thought was open, stunned and thrown right back to where she was with him two months prior.

"Hi," he said coolly, bringing her in for a hug with his whole body. Like her, he wore a beanie but otherwise no disguise, risking being spotted and outed as a celebrity. She didn't care as long as she could see his eyes. Her legs threatened to give in as she melted deeper into the hug.

"Hi," she squeaked out onto his collarbone. More words threatened to break free, but she no longer had the emotional capacity to slow them if they decided to unleash.

She pulled back as he picked up her bag, catching her arms to hold her in front of him. Invisible lightning strikes seemed to shoot between their eyes, exchanging energy.

"I'm so happy to see you," he said, so genuinely she had to look away. "Let's get going. We'll be running out of sunlight soon and Aunt Rita is dying to meet you."

"How's she doing?" Tess asked, curious, but desperate to distract herself from the way she felt right now.

"She's alright. Better, for sure. But she'll kill me if I keep you to myself." He threw her bag in the back of the car. They hopped in and took off, back up the coast to Halifax.

The car ride was annoying normal. They'd only been apart for two months, and Henry didn't know about the enormous change in Tess's life that was about to upend his. Still, it felt odd to talk about music and trivial happenings since they'd last been together. They'd never been superficial, and the lack of depth of the first hour of their car ride kept Tess's focus out the window, unable to really look him in the face. It wasn't clear if he was being purposefully distant, or if they really had lost a degree of intimacy without communicating for so long.

"So how was it for you?" he finally asked, seemingly tired of the vacant pleasantries.

"How was what for me?"

"Coming home? I'll say, for me it was rough. Not coming home, but you going home. Turns out Abzac is not as lovely as it was with you. Especially when you've found yourself unexpectedly heartbroken."

Heartbroken. That was the best word for it, but she hadn't planned on divulging much about how miserable she'd been. About how her friends had to drag her out of bed some days and force burritos down her throat. They had known leaving each other would be hard, and commiserating on it just felt like it would mean they'd have to do it again after this trip.

"Yeah, it was a lot at once. I'd say rough, too. Really great to be with Maria and Jo though. I needed them."

He seemed to sense her protecting herself and did not press. "Do you want to hear the new record?" he asked, cheekily. He was so lovely when he was proud of himself, and Tess admired the confidence he had in his work.

She smiled and nodded. "Anything I might recognize?"

"Maybe," he said, as he pulled the file up on his phone. The first track started with their familiar *"dada da da, da dada da da."*

Tess closed her eyes, still smiling, and promptly fell deeply asleep.

The setting sun beamed into her face as she awoke to being lightly stroked on the arm. She'd slept the entire rest of the way to the house.

"Shit, Henry, I'm so sorry. I can't believe I...I just—"

"No worries, darling. You've had a long day. But you better snap into the Tess I know—it's cocktail hour!" he said as he pushed the door open, jogging around the car to come open her side.

Aunt Rita's "cottage," as he'd described it to her, looked more like a chalet. It wasn't huge, but it was gorgeous, like a hidden treasure amid huge pine trees sprinkled around the large property. A full window wall looked out past the immaculate garden onto the rocky beach below. Even the small guest house in the back would be a dream house for most. Tess innately understood the magic of this place, experiencing awe to the fullest extent.

"Ready to meet Aunt Rita?" Henry asked as if it were a real question. He took her hand and led her toward the mahogany double entry doors.

He was letting her in, even further than she'd already been with him.

Twenty-four

Aunt Rita was lovely. It was no surprise that she'd been so close with Antoinette—they had the same salt-of-the-earthness about them. Rita was more feminine, and her perfect posture and sharp jaw suggested that she would not be messed with. She also shared Henry's warmth—a prized familial trait—and pulled Tess in for a hug at first meeting.

"Lovely to meet you, dear. I've heard so much," Rita cooed into Tess's hair, holding on tight to her hug with this stranger.

"Same to you!" Tess responded, slightly more emotional about the meeting than she would have been able to explain.

Henry beamed from Tess's side, clearly tickled that two women he cared for were coming together. Tess wondered how she'd been described to Rita, what she knew about the two of them, and how many other nameless Tesses she'd been introduced to over the years.

"Tess is exhausted from the trip—but I'm sure she's hungry. Wine, everyone?" Henry offered, disappearing into the kitchen before waiting for a response.

Shit. Tess had not thought this one through, scrambling to come up with a good enough, nonchalant reason as to why she would not be drinking. She came up blank and resolved to hold the full glass all night without revealing that she wasn't actually drinking it.

Rita and Antoinette must have grown up going to dinner parties together. Both women knew how to pull out all the stops for a guest, without making it seem any different than any other ordinary night of the week. The table was covered with holly sprigs and pinecones and berries Rita must have picked up from her property. Natural, effortless, yet elegant.

"Your house is so beautiful," Tess offered, looking around as she made her way to the table. It had a Scandinavian feel of modernity, even within the historic wood framing. The design was very particular but somehow made Tess feel at home right away. Beautiful as a piece of artwork, yet cozy.

"It's my temple, really. I don't have children, so I have to direct all my fussing somewhere. Especially when I don't see this guy very much." She nodded toward Henry.

"Well, now you can't get rid of me," he said, winking as he handed out the long-stemmed glasses. Tess brought the glass to her lips as a habit, before faking a cough to set it back down. This was going to be harder than she thought.

Rita rolled her eyes with a smile, proving that Henry's charm had no bounds. "I'm much more interested in hearing about you, Tess. Henry tells me he's never met anyone like you before and insisted that I meet you." She landed her sentence without a question, leaving Tess fumbling over how to respond to such an unclear, assumed compliment.

"Oh, that can't be true. He's been all over the world and met so many people! I'm very regular," she insisted, catching Henry shaking his head "no" out of her periphery.

"This is what he says. He says I need to know how you see the world," Rita continued, narrowing her eyes on Tess as if to say she meant business. Leave it to Henry to prepare the most important person in his world to cut past the get-to-know-you bullshit and head straight for the heart.

"How I see the world, huh?" Tess side-glanced at him as he took a giant swig from his wine. "That sure is a big topic. Care to explain, Henry? I'm going to need more specifics to divulge my entire worldview."

"Well, if you must know, I was talking to Rita about the way you see me. How it's just one example of the way you see everyone and everything. Mostly the goodness. And the way you question things. You know, it had a major impact on me in the short time that I've known you," he added, clearing his throat and resuming drinking.

"Ah. Yes, I guess the thing to know about me is I see a lot of goodness. In people, situations, environments. I've spent a lot of time navigating to the core of who I really am and what feels really true to me. I'm a writer, and that's what I write about. It's a bit hard to explain without sounding like I am a perky, privileged, happy-go-lucky person. Goodness is just one of those things I can't give up on in anyone, ever."

Rita nodded, holding her gaze. Tess slightly flushed knowing all eyes were on her as she revealed her most vulnerable beliefs.

"Hold on to that, Tess," Rita advised. "Don't apologize for it. It's a beautiful thing to believe, and only good can come from that. Share that with the world. Only good can come from *that*. And you're right, my Henry is good. I'm glad you've been able to help him see that," she added, continuing the practice of intense eye contact she'd clearly imparted to Henry.

Tess nodded, noting that she did, often, try to downplay these feelings, like she was embarrassed that this was what she believed. Here, with Henry and Rita, it felt like a superpower. They saw her how she wanted to be seen, as she truly was, and helped strip some of the shame away from how she saw herself.

Throughout dinner Tess picked up her wine glass at least half a dozen times without thinking, and even took a sip twice, to her own panic. The Cornish pasties Rita made looked amazing and normally would have been Tess's dream dinner. The baby, however, was not a fan. Nausea got the best of her, and she fought it down with tiny bites and sips of water, talking as much as she could to distract from her lack of eating and drinking like a normal person.

Rita was easy to get talking. A fairly simple question could get her going, and a small probe would launch into a detailed, twenty-minute retelling of her time as a teacher. The man named Liam whom she almost married before realizing she never really wanted to get married at all. The time her tomatoes were infested by blister beetles. Tess commiserated, wondering if Antoinette had called Rita to complain about Tess's beetle blunder that summer.

"I don't know where you live, Tess?" Rita asked. Tess wondered if there was a motive, or encouragement from Henry to ask such a boring question, leading into a discussion of why their summer romance had to end.

"That's a great question, actually. I'm currently staying with a friend in Maine. Before that, I was in New York, with another friend. I lived in Maryland before I left for the summer and haven't really settled on where I'll end up after this transient period. The new book has me traveling all over right now, so there's no real point in settling anywhere. I do really love the northeast, though, so Portland is certainly a contender for my next home."

Henry's eyebrow shot up, as this was news to him.

"What about your family?" Rita asked. It was a valid follow-up question, but one without a simple answer Tess could offer a near-stranger. She sipped her wine slowly, letting it run through her mouth and back into the glass to buy time.

"Not in the picture," Henry said, saving her from an answer she didn't have. Rita, like Henry, seemed to be able to sense when to pry and when not to.

"Sorry to hear that. Cake?" Rita offered.

"Yes, please," Henry and Tess answered in unison, matching smiles as their eyes met.

The night was still young, but the pitch-black sky outside and Rita's continued rehabilitation had her retiring to the guest house by eight o'clock. She'd cupped Tess's face in her hands before kissing both cheeks. "I am so pleased to meet you, Tess. I look forward to seeing you in the morning. Thank you for coming all this way. For both of us," she added.

Once alone, Henry and Tess's dance of pretending to be friends continued. Tess sat in a large armchair, cradling the still-full wine she'd had all night as Henry lit a fire. The muscles in his forearm flexed as he picked up the wood, and Tess ached to be held by those arms. She'd tried before to maintain her distance from this man, unsuccessfully. Tonight, she resolved to stay in her armchair where it was safe.

Something harkening to her hunter-gatherer ancestors made it incredibly attractive to watch a man make a fire. His soft blow under the wood sparked the flame so it caught, as did Tess's breath. She turned her attention out the window in an effort to distract herself by the phenomenon of snow falling on the beach.

With his hands on his hips, Henry let out a triumphant "hmph!", pleased with himself. He stepped back from his precious fire and took a seat on the sofa across from her.

"This is weird," he said, mimicking his sentiment from their phone conversation.

"Yeah. I don't really know how to be around you like this." Which was absolutely true. They'd arrived at the part of the evening where she had to calmly, without pressure, disclose the most important life-changing news of his life. *In two- three-four, out two-three-four.*

"Tell me about the music," she tried, changing the topic.

"Well, for some people it's a real sleeper." He winked. "But I am incredibly proud. It feels like the truest album I've made so far. And, as you'd probably guess, there's a lot of you in that."

She pursed her lips to prevent her smile from giving her away, instead shaking her head with her hands on her cheeks. "I can't believe I fell asleep. I swear, I've been so excited to hear how it came out. If you'd just give me another shot, I promise my attention will be—"

"Tess!" he yelled and leaped toward her. She jumped up in a panic, feeling the heat at her leg at the same time.

The hem of her sweater was on fire. He smacked her thigh, right on the flame, and extinguished it immediately. They both stared at the spot where the fire had been, where her hem was left singed, and burst into laughter.

"Are you okay? That was wild! An ember must have jumped out at you."

"I'm fine," she promised. "It was just my sweater. You have some really intense reflexes. The way you jumped I'd have thought the whole house was on fire."

"Instinct, I suppose. Had to protect you."

"Of course," she laughed, realizing how close they were standing. He raised his hand to her waist, and she lifted hers to his chest. They stood for a minute, eyes closed, connecting again by such minimal touch.

Before she could open her eyes, his lips were on hers. She knew herself now, and she definitely knew herself with Henry. If they started down this road she would not stop. Her hands found his face and pulled him back from her. She couldn't bear to say it out loud but begged him with her eyes. That she didn't know if she could survive it again. Her eyes burned.

He listened to what she did not say, shaking his head, as if to counter her plea. "Look, Tess. I'm sorry. I don't know how to do this. You know how I feel. I can't be around you and pretend."

It was truly too much. In her hormonal, emotionally drained state she could not prevent the truth from pouring out of her mouth.

"I love you, Henry," she gushed. Rehearsed conversation be damned, she was way off script.

He pulled her in and held her in such a way that she could feel his heart through his arms. Tight enough to feel loved, supported, known. Loose enough to feel free, untethered, individual. He loved her, and now he knew that she felt the same. Even in the blur of his touch and cacophony of emotions that whirred around her head like hummingbirds, Tess knew she had to press on to the real conversation before she lost her nerve. She pulled back to look at him.

"I didn't just come here to see you because I miss you. I...I came here to tell you something important. I don't...I can't..." She stepped back, shaking her head, coming up empty as if she'd forgotten the English language completely. She was not going to be able to present this as tactfully as she planned. "Wait here," she said, heading back to her bag to pull out her backup plan.

She returned with the plastic stick in her palm. A look of recognition lit up in his eyes as she got close enough for him to see what she was holding.

He looked at the test. Back at her. Back to the test.

"Two blue lines," he said, a new tear breaking free from his eye.

"Before you say anything I need you to know that I have considered all *my* options. I have had an abortion in the past. After that, I thought I might not actually want kids. But Henry...I want to have this baby. I can't explain it, I just know it's the right thing for me."

They breathed in unison.

"I realize that is an enormous decision for both of us. I don't expect anything from you—and I mean that wholeheartedly. The last thing I want to do is take away your choices and ruin your career and change the course of your life. But for me, somehow, I *know* I want to have this baby. Please, don't say anything yet. I just had to come here to tell you." The speech she had so meticulously planned came out in fragmented shards as she braced for the silence. His wide eyes found their way to hers.

"Yes," he stated, almost matter-of-factly, unwavering.

"Henry—"

"*Yes*," he repeated, more insistently. His face held total seriousness.

"No. This hasn't even sunk in yet. You can't just hear life-altering news and immediately agree to throw away your future. However you want to be involved or not is a huge decision."

"I know. I say yes."

"There is so much to consider here for you. This isn't just a momentary decision, this is *parenthood*. And I have nothing figured out. I don't even know where I'm going to live, or how any of this is going to work. You're going on tour soon—"

"Fuck the tour. You and I both know I'm not really built for a public life. I wanted an out, but this isn't just an out for me," he blurted out, impassioned, so fierce he almost sounded angry. His eye contact was so intense and genuine that she couldn't bear to blink and miss a second of it. Henry softened his tone and continued. "Look, I tried to go back to my regular life, but it's bullshit. It's not what I want. I love you, Tess. I *want* to be with you, and everything that entails. I don't need time; I don't need to process. I know exactly what I want. If you want to do this, and if you want to do this with me? I am in. I am all in."

She could not get her mouth to close. Nowhere in any version of the plan for her life did she envision this. Tess, lover of playbooks and rules. Logic and rationale and sensibility had been the pillars of every decision she had made for thirty years. Yet here, in this absolute upheaval of her life and plans and goals, the feelings took over. At the crux of Tess's logic and Henry's feeling was the hope of the tiny seed growing inside her.

Leading with her heart, Tess took his beautiful face in her hands and kissed him. They sat for minutes in one deep kiss, saying nothing, but telling each other everything.

They finally pulled away, both breathless. Several words rolled around in her mouth before Tess was able to let out a comprehensive thought. When it did come, it surprised her too.

"So, what do we do?"

August, again

Twenty-five

Tess's eyes fluttered open to her phone buzzing as the late morning Halifax sun streamed in through the gap in the curtains. She blinked several times as her pupils adjusted to the light out the window. Even in six months, she had not gotten used to this view. The sun dancing on the Atlantic Ocean. The sandpipers hopping around on the beach. Their beach. It still hit her like a ton of bricks. *This is my life. I live here.*

Her phone vibrated again, her mom's name popping up at the top of the text bubble. Her parents' flight had been delayed half an hour.

Sorry, honey. See you soon.

A smile dancing on her lips, Tess sat buzzing with the excitement of their impending visit. To hug her mom. To hear her dad call her "kid".

She stretched her legs out and her arms up, sending a tingle of excitement through her limbs, enveloping her whole body.

Edith Piaf's familiar voice carried into the room, muffled by the door. Eager to join on the other side, Tess pulled on her robe, plunged her toes into her slippers and meandered out of the room.

Henry was swaying in the kitchen, humming, rocking their daughter in his arms. His eye caught hers as he turned, and every muscle in his face teamed up to form a wide, genuine smile. She could not help but match his.

"Lookit, Sunny, Mummy's up! We wanted to let you rest a bit, darling, so we're working on our French out here. Rita and Antoinette just left for the Farmer's Market." Tess nodded, still smiling, reveling in the sight of them.

Tonight, they would all be together, eating curry at their long table by candlelight. Rita and Antoinette, Tess's parents, Tess and Henry and the magic they made in tiny human form. A mosaic of the life they were building.

Henry turned his back to her so Tess could see the baby, just over a month old, peeking over his bare shoulder with dark eyes like her mama and a hint of Henry's curls. Tess moved toward them and kissed him, then their daughter's head, then his shoulder again.

"There is nothing I want that I don't have," she breathed into his skin. Tess wrapped her arms around them, resting her cheek on his shoulder, lips pressed to her baby's head. All three swaying to the music. Dancing in front of their fireplace, Tess's painting hanging over the mantle. A family.

Her Henry and their sunbeam, Sunny.

Acknowledgements

As with all projects near and dear to the artist's heart, this has been a labor of love. Not only by me and my love of writing, incessant imagination and inability to yield to the inconvenience of having big dreams. The love that fueled this labor was sparked by my dearest friends and family.

First and foremost, I have to thank Maura and Lindsay. You two truly made this happen, in all literal and metaphorical ways. Thank you for letting me borrow inspiration from our sisterhood. Thank you for your absolute, full-throttle, often blind support of me in everything, especially this. I am who I am today because of you and I am so grateful.

Lauren, my lifelong best friend. I love you for loving this book before knowing anything about it. And for planning your outfit for the book launch party well before the book existed.

Brooke and Dad. Your beta-reading and positive encouragement pulled me out of a time when I didn't know if any of this had been worth it. You both love so big, and I'm so lucky you love me.

Mom. Thank you for fostering my imagination and creativity, passing down your tenacity, and laminating cardboard covers of books I wrote when I was five. Thank you for reading this and editing this and correcting my French and doing it all again and again until it was good. Sorry I ignored all your pleas to remove profanity.

Ariana, my sister. Your cover design is gorgeous, and the tenacity *you* got from Mom made it perfect. Your word suggestions and hearts and smilies marked throughout the first manuscript gave me hope that people might read this and even like it. Thank you for being my sister and my friend.

Margot and Jude, my darlings. Thank you for mostly napping so mommy could write, and never pressing "delete all" when you bang on my keyboard. I love you when you are convenient and I love you when you're not.

Finally, my Mac. The epitome of a partner. Thank you for giving me time, space and pickup of my parenting slack to pursue this dream. For believing in me in *everything* I do. For your genuine excitement. Writing this book has made me extra grateful that we are who we are after twelve years and so much change, and I am stupid lucky that you are the one I chose when I was just a kid.

Author's Note

Writing a book has always been a dream of mine. It felt like one of those too-big dreams you don't know how to start.

One day I just started writing, bringing to life an idea I had for a cheeky love story, full of French loveliness and a fairly specific British love interest. Maybe you would call it fanfic.

What evolved has become so much more important to me.

I wrote Tess with so many precious bits of myself that it almost felt too personal to publish by the end. Pieces of her journey, specifically reimagining her beliefs, came from my own experience in deconstruction.

I participated in a sect of American evangelicalism for most of my teen to adult life. Many of those years were spent actively evangelizing young people into this belief system, teaching what I believed to be true. When I finally allowed myself to ask questions, I found that none of it sat right with me.

Always ask questions.

To me, belief is best laid on a foundation of what feels right and good to you and doesn't hurt anyone else. Personally, I had to extract myself from a belief system laid out for me. Who I am now is myself—the most comfortable, truest version I have ever been.

I have some amazing friends—two of whom inspired characters in this book—and a loving partner who fiercely supported me along the way. I hold tightly to the belief that we are wired for community.

My hope for you, dear reader, is that you are comfortable with who you are and what you believe, that you know what feels right and good to you. That you have the freedom to follow your heart rather than a rulebook for life. And that you would give others space to do the same.

I wrote this book so that you would know you are not alone.